Chased by the Alpha

DEVIL SPRINGS

BOOK TWO

C.C. WOOD

For Mom, who unknowingly sparked my love of romance novels. I snuck all your Harlequins and read them when I was probably too young. But it inspired my dream of writing about people falling in love.
Happy Birthday and I miss you.

Prologue

My tires squealed as I pulled off the road and braked hard.

I barely took the time to kill the ignition and lock the car before I bolted to the trees nearby, unbuttoning my jeans as I moved.

As soon as I was out of sight of the road, I ran around a tree, yanked my pants down, and squatted.

Oh, my God, why did I have to buy the biggest iced coffee during my last pit stop? I knew I would have to pee. I just knew it.

But did that stop me? Noooo.

After what seemed like an eternity, I was finally done. I dug a couple of napkins out of my pocket and used them to clean up.

Thank goodness I'd grabbed some during that stop. And that I had hand sanitizer in the car.

I carefully got to my feet and pulled up my pants, stepping away from the tree.

I hoped Devil Springs wasn't too much further. I'd likely have to pee again in another half hour or so. Damned iced coffee.

The navigation app I had on my phone wasn't helpful at all. It was giving me directions to Devil Springs but kept glitching on the time and distance. One minute it would say ten miles and twenty minutes until arrival. The next it would say three hundred miles and two minutes to arrival. I finally turned off the annoying voice that kept telling me that shit and just followed the directions. They seemed to be leading me to the right place because I'd just passed a sign that said Devil Springs-10 miles a few moments before I had to pull off the road.

I tried to wait. I really did. But my bladder wasn't having it.

Just as I was about to head back toward my car, the sound of snapping twigs and something large moving through the trees distracted me.

I froze. That sounded like an animal. A big one. Were bears this far south? Mountain lions? Oh, God, was something stalking me and planning to have me for lunch?

I took a few steps deeper into the woods, peeking around a huge tree, and froze when I saw a huge wolf. The creature was bigger than any wolf I'd ever seen before.

Almost as big as a black bear.

Holy crap! I didn't think wolves even lived in this region, much less that I'd run into one during a pee break.

Before I could take a step back and silently head back to my car, the wolf shook itself violently.

Then, the weirdest thing happened.

Its fur began to recede, and its body began to ripple and change. It was like watching a train wreck or childbirth, horrifying but it was something you couldn't stop staring at.

A canine moan came from its mouth, morphing into a human groan of pain as it shifted from four legs to two.

In a few seconds, the giant wolf had become an equally giant man. A huge, naked man.

I blinked rapidly, my brain trying to process what I was seeing.

This couldn't be real. I must have finally managed to OD on caffeine. That was the only acceptable explanation—caffeine-induced hallucinations.

My only other option was that I was having another mental breakdown.

I took a tiny step back and, damn my shitty luck, my heel landed right on a twig.

Snap!

CHASED BY THE ALPHA

Oh, shit. Oh, shit. I froze again. I'd read somewhere that human eyes tracked movement so maybe he wouldn't see me if I stayed still.

He was too far away for me to see his eye color, but I knew the moment he caught sight of me.

His body tensed and I saw every bulky muscle swell. He swung toward me and—holy mother of God, his dick was just as big as the rest of him!

I didn't hesitate after that.

I whirled around and sprinted through the trees back toward my car, yanking the keys from my pocket as I went and hitting the button for the remote start over and over until I heard the sound of a distant horn honking twice.

I could hear the man crashing through the trees behind me. He was already too close. I could tell.

Crap.

I poured on more speed, calling for every ounce I could wrench from my legs. I think this was the fastest I'd run since I won the 100-yard dash in my district track meet in high school. I'd won first place, so maybe I had a shot.

The trees were thinning around me, and I was relieved when I saw that my car was just ahead.

I swore I felt hot breath on my neck as I burst out of the woods and practically vaulted over the hood of my car like an action movie star.

I had to jerk the door handle twice before it finally opened and I all but dove inside. I slammed the door shut and put the car in gear, my foot already on the accelerator.

The engine roared and the tires smoked as I peeled away from the shoulder, driving like a bat out of hell toward what I hoped was Devil Springs.

Only then did I look in the rearview mirror.

My heart nearly stopped when I saw the naked hulking man running after my car.

And I wasn't leaving him behind even though I was going nearly forty miles per hour.

I jammed my foot down on the gas pedal until it hit the floor. The

3

speedometer read sixty-five before he began to fall back. Then, once I hit eighty miles per hour, I looked in the mirror again and he was gone.

A hysterical laugh bubbled up out of my throat.

Had I just been chased through the woods by a naked werewolf in his human form? Or had I hallucinated the entire thing?

Maybe I was really cracking up.

I gripped the steering wheel harder as I urged the car to go faster. No, no, I wasn't cracking up. I was just exhausted. I'd been working too much and not sleeping enough.

I wasn't crazy. I only needed a break. A nice vacation with my friend. And a chance to meet this mystery man that she'd fallen so in love with that she was moving halfway across the country for him.

This time, my fingers gripped the steering wheel harder out of concern rather than fear.

He better work his ass off to deserve my bestie or they would never, ever find his body.

In the distance, I saw buildings. There was a sign to my right that read, "Welcome to Devil Springs."

I laughed to myself.

"Hey, Devil Springs. I doubt you're ready for me."

Chapter One

I tried to ignore the way my hands were shaking as I steered my car down the main street of Devil Springs.

A sign reading Devil Springs Grocery caught my eye. That was the name of Cari's store. Well, her great-aunt's store, but she inherited it after Bethany died.

I pulled into a parking spot and put the car in park. My heart was still racing from the...hallucination I had in the woods.

I needed to calm down.

I let my hands slide from the wheel to rest in my lap and focused on my breathing. In and out. In and out. Slow and deep.

I couldn't say anything about this to anyone. They would think I was nuts. Just like my parents had.

"I'm not losing it," I whispered. "I'm just stressed and tired. Sometimes people see things that aren't there when they're exhausted. Nothing happened."

One more deep breath and I knew I had to get out of the driver's seat, or I'd still be sitting here when Cari closed her store and came outside.

Bracing myself, I shut off the car and grabbed my purse.

The air was cool and fresh as I locked the car, letting my head swivel to take in the downtown area of Devil Springs. Despite the fact that the town was small, nearly every parking space was filled, and people strolled along the sidewalks with paper cups of coffee or shopping bags in their hands.

It was so pretty and picturesque that it almost didn't seem real.

I never would have imagined that Cari would want to stay here, but it was exactly the kind of place I'd always wanted to live. A place where everyone knew everyone else, neighbors helped each other, and there were annual events that brought the townsfolk together.

I smiled to myself as I entered the grocery and the antique bell over the door clanked.

And I stepped right into utter mayhem.

"Close the door!" Cari shouted from somewhere behind a tall shelf. I couldn't see her, but I knew the sound of her voice.

Claws scrabbled on the hardwood floor as a huge, fluffy puppy made its way toward the open door behind me.

Moving quickly, I shut the door and scooped up the pup, noting the package of peanut butter cups hanging from its mouth.

"Hey there, cutie," I cooed. "That's not good for you. It'll make you sick."

I tried to be gentle and remove the candy from the puppy's mouth, but it growled and tried to shake the package from my grip.

"Leave it," I said, making my voice sharp and putting a little pressure on the back of the puppy's jaw.

It growled again but dropped the candy into my waiting hand.

I tossed the orange package on the old-fashioned wooden counter to my left and turned the puppy in my arms, holding it like a baby.

It yelped and tried to scrabble out of my arms, but I put a hand on its belly and rubbed a few gentle circles.

"It's okay, baby. You're safe with me," I said as I rocked the puppy. "I won't hurt you."

It blinked up at me, its gaze wide but not as scared as it had been a few seconds before. I hummed beneath my breath as I kept rubbing its belly, noticing that it was definitely a boy pup.

"It's okay, little dude. Who do you belong to?" I murmured, glancing at the puppy's neck to see if it wore a collar.

Nothing.

Huh. The puppy was clean and well-fed, clearly taken care of, yet no collar. That was strange. Even stranger is that it looked quite a bit like a wolf.

After a few more seconds of me staring into the pup's eyes, it went limp in my arms with a little groan, wiggling closer to my chest.

"Aw, you're such a sweet baby," I said. "If you don't already belong to someone, you can come home with me."

The puppy's tongue came out to lick my forearm before his head rolled back and he panted with a smile, his tongue now hanging out the side of his mouth.

It was such a cute look that I had to laugh.

"Sela?" Cari asked.

I looked up to find my friend gaping at me as though she'd just seen a ghost.

"Hey, girlie. Surprise!" I said, still petting the pup.

Cari approached slowly. "What are you doing here?"

Pain pinched my chest. She didn't seem all that excited to see me. The backs of my eyes stung, threatening tears.

"I missed you," I answered simply, hugging the puppy closer. "And I wanted to meet your new guy in person instead of just on video."

The puppy snuggled deeper into my arms, sighing again and licking my neck.

Cari was still staring at me as though she couldn't believe her eyes.

"Should I leave? Is this a bad surprise?" I asked, the pain in my chest spreading to encompass my entire torso.

The question seemed to shake her out of her stupor. "What? No! You need to stay!"

"Then, why don't you seem happy to see me?"

Her expression softened. "I am happy to see you." She paused. "It's just that..." She trailed off as though she wasn't sure what to say but gestured to the ball of fur in my arms.

"Puppy?" I supplied.

"Yes. He's half-wild, but he seems to have taken to you."

I grinned at her. "He's a sweetie pie. Do you know who owns him? He's not even wearing a collar! What kind of parents let their furbaby run around with no collar?"

Cari made a choking sound, but before she could respond, the door behind me opened, hitting me in the shoulder.

I grunted in shock and stumbled forward. I glanced over my shoulder to see what in the hell came through the door because I was pretty sure I was going to have a bruise down one side of my body.

Then, my mouth fell open.

It was the man I saw in the woods. Or the man I thought I imagined in the woods. And he was even bigger up close than I thought.

Oh, my God. I'd hallucinated. Hadn't I? This couldn't be real.

He wedged himself through the door and shut it behind him, the antique bell over the top clanging when it slammed.

My eyes were locked on his and I couldn't look away.

His blue-green eyes seemed to brighten, and his pupils expanded as he inhaled deeply, still staring at me.

A low growl rumbled from his chest.

I took a step back, my back hitting the wooden counter. What the fuck? Did he just growl at me like a fucking animal? My brain was moving too fast. I couldn't focus on a single thought other than the fact that this man was the same man I'd thought I saw in the woods.

The puppy in my arms cringed and burrowed deeper into my arms. I clutched him tighter, running a soothing hand over his back as he turned his belly toward me.

"Sheriff Stoic, so nice to see you today," Cari said, coming closer.

The big guy stared at me for one more second before he turned to my friend. She seemed unfazed by his intensity and the growl.

Now that I wasn't entranced by his pretty greenish blue eyes, I took the rest of him in. He was massive. At least six-four and built like a linebacker. His golden blond hair was buzzed around his neck but longer on top and it had a hint of curl. His skin was fair, but the back of his neck was tinged pink, as though he'd gotten too much sun. He looked like he could be dropped onto the set of one of those Viking shows my ex used to watch and fit right in.

"I told you not to call me that," he rumbled at Cari. "I'm the police chief, not a sheriff."

Cari grinned at him, her eyes sparkling with mischief.

Well, he couldn't be as big of an asshole as he seemed if she was comfortable enough to tease him like that.

I was shaken though. First, I thought I saw him change from a wolf into a human in the woods and now here he was, growling at me like a damn dog.

God, I had imagined all of that happening in the woods, right? Because werewolves weren't a thing. They're fiction. Hot fiction if the romance novels I liked to read were any indication, but fiction nonetheless.

"So you have," Cari quipped. She gestured toward the pup I was holding. "Bo's back up to his old tricks."

Aw, the puppy's name was Bo. How cute was that?

The puppy cringed when the man turned toward me, his gaze landing first on my face, then on the furball in my arms.

The police chief took a step toward me, reaching for the puppy.

Bo whined against my neck, his cold, wet nose pressing hard into my skin.

I turned away from the chief's reaching hands, shielding the dog with my body. "You're scaring him."

The enormous man stopped, staring at me in surprise, as though he couldn't believe I had the temerity to defy him.

His green-blue eyes glittered at me. "He's not scared of me. He's scared of what his parents will do when I drop him off at home."

Bo whined pitifully against my skin again, all but climbing me in an effort to hide from the big man.

I squinted at him. "I'm not sure I believe you. Why would he be acting like this if he didn't know you and didn't fear you? Have you harmed this dog before?"

The police chief's eyes widened at my words, and I heard Cari snort as she tried to stifle her laugh.

"I would never harm a pup of my—"

Cari cleared her throat abruptly and the chief stopped speaking. He took a deep breath, closing his eyes as he released it. When he opened them again, they didn't glitter quite as brightly.

"I don't hurt babies of any species," he grumbled, his voice deep.

He stood so close to me that I could almost feel the vibration of his

9

words against my arms. We were only a few inches apart and my skin tingled as though a mild electrical current hit me.

I slid my eyes toward Cari for verification.

"He's a good man," she said, an evil grin spreading across her face.

I sighed. She was enjoying this way too much, which had to mean that the police chief was a good guy. If he was an asshole, she would have tried to get rid of him as soon as possible instead of teasing him.

"What's your name?" he asked.

He didn't move but I suddenly had the impression he was much closer.

I lifted my chin. He was trying to intimidate me, but I wasn't going to fall for that. Scarier men than him had tried. Well, maybe not scarier, but men had tried to make me bow down before and it hadn't worked then. It wasn't going to work now either.

"I'm Sela Harper. Who are you?"

"Garrett Kent. I'm the police chief here in Devil Springs."

Our gazes clashed, neither of us backing down.

Until Cari burst out laughing.

We both turned to her. "What?"

I shot him a narrow-eyed glare when he spoke in unison with me.

"I just never thought I'd meet anyone who wasn't intimidated by Sela," she said. "Or a woman who wasn't terrified of Sheriff Stoic."

I bit back my smile as the police chief sighed, resignation clear on his face. Obviously, my friend's little nickname for him wasn't a new thing.

He faced me. His eyes were no longer on me but on the puppy in my arms.

"Bo, you know you're not supposed to be here without your parents. Quit hiding behind Sela and let me take you home."

I frowned at the police chief. No, Garrett. If I thought of him as the police chief, I would let him get to me. I respected law enforcement officers and tried to be kind because God knew what kind of crap they had to put up with day in and day out. If I thought about it, I'd soften toward him and that wasn't going to happen.

To my shock, the puppy seemed to understand his words because it wiggled in my arms until it faced Garrett, who was holding his huge hands out toward me, a patient expression on his face.

Not toward me. Toward the puppy.

Grudgingly, I handed the dog over and tried not to stare as Garrett cupped the dog's tiny butt in one hand and supported his upper body with another, lifting him to face level.

"You can't keep coming in here and doing this, Bo. It's not how honorable wolves behave."

That dog was actually a wolf? My eyes widened. Wow, I was lucky he hadn't bitten me. He must have been with humans since birth for him to be so sweet and friendly.

Bo whined and licked Garrett's nose. Living up to his nickname, Sheriff Stoic didn't even crack a smile.

Garrett glanced at Cari. "I'll have a chat with his parents again," he said.

That was kind of cute, the way he kept referring to the puppy's owners as his "parents."

No. Not cute. Sheriff Stoic was rude. And had apparently starred in my crazy imagination before I'd even met him.

God, I couldn't think about that right now. I couldn't even process it. I'd seen a lot of strange things in my life, but I'd learned never to talk about them because no one ever believed me.

Cari nodded and crossed her arms over her chest. "Thanks, Garrett."

He looked at me one more time. "I'll see you around, Sela Harper."

"Or not," I snarked back.

He just smirked at me before leaving the store with the fluffy puppy perched on his chest.

I tried to ignore how hot he looked holding the dog, but it was a losing battle. The sight of a big man holding a tiny, fluffy puppy just did something to me.

When the door shut behind him, there was a rush of feet and suddenly Cari's arms were around me.

"It's so good to see you," she mumbled against my shoulder. She was nearly half a foot shorter than me, so I hugged her to my chest like a little kid.

"I missed you," I murmured back, resting my cheek on her hair.

This was the welcome I'd been hoping for when I started my drive to Devil Springs, Texas.

Cari pulled back and looked up at me. "How long are you here?"

I shrugged, dropping my arms. Hug time was over, it seemed.

"I had a ton of vacation built up, so I'm taking a month with the option of another week or two of either vacation or half days depending on if they need me at work or not."

"A whole month?" Cari asked, her eyes lighting up.

Then, her face fell.

"I don't have to stay the whole time," I said, reading the change in her mood. "I know you just shacked up with Daniel and y'all are in the golden honeymoon glow and everything."

"It's not that," she answered, but she didn't elaborate.

Ouch. She was killing me. Maybe this was a mistake after all.

"We'll play it by ear."

Now, I was rethinking my hope that I could stay with her. Her attitude was hurting my feelings. A lot. It had been several months since we'd seen each other, and she was acting as though I was a nuisance rather than her best friend.

"So, where are the best hotels around here?" I asked.

My question shook Cari out of her thoughts. "You're not staying at a hotel! You can stay at Bethany's cottage. All her furniture is still there, and I just went through and dusted the place last week."

"Won't I be in the way if you and Daniel are there?"

"Oh, I'm living with Daniel in his house outside of town."

The words hung between us.

So, I wasn't welcome to stay with her at Daniel's. That hurt.

The bell over the door rang again and two women came in and grabbed shopping carts, glancing at us with open curiosity.

No, not us. Me.

Crap, this was a bad idea. Maybe I should have just stayed in Tennessee. It never occurred to me that my best friend wouldn't be as excited to see me as I was to see her.

"I have to help these ladies," Cari murmured. "Let me get you the key to the cottage." She paused. "I can't hang out right now, but how about you come to the house for dinner tonight? We can catch up and you can see that Daniel is actually a decent guy."

I hid the hurt I was feeling because it wasn't Cari's fault or even her problem. She fell in love. I was glad that she was happy.

But I couldn't help feeling like I was being cast aside.

Cari disappeared through the door behind the antique wooden counter, and I took a moment to look around the store. Wow, it was larger than I expected based on the exterior. The inside was a charming mix of old world and modern conveniences. The shelves that held pantry items, canned goods, and cleaning products were all heavy, dark wood and obviously antiques.

Yet there was a refrigerated area along the back wall that held milk, dairy, eggs, and meat. There was a free-standing freezer with double doors that held ice cream and some other frozen items.

There was even a small section of clothing and shoes near the register.

Overall, I loved the vibe of this store. It fit right in with the entire atmosphere of Devil Springs that I'd seen so far. Small town that was both modern but still nostalgic.

I was a little bit envious.

Cari had not only found a man that she loved, she had slotted right into the kind of life I'd always wanted for myself.

I'd dreamed of owning a small business in a town where everyone knew me and where I had friends and family who didn't give me side-long glances or walk on eggshells around me.

A place where I could completely be myself without having to watch every little thing I said because it might lead to arguments about my "overactive imagination" as it had when I was younger.

Or the concerned looks that never quite went away when I was in my parents' home. As though they were waiting for me to fall apart.

Cari returned with a key ring in her hand. "The cottage is just behind the grocery store. If you go down to the next street and turn right, it's the first house on the right." She handed me a sticky note with the address written on it. "Just so you can be sure you're at the right spot."

One of the women started coming over, a big jar in her hand.

"I have to help these customers, but I'll text you with a time and our address for dinner tonight, okay?" she said, already distracted.

"Sure."

Cari hugged me one more time. "I really am glad you're here. Take some time to walk around the town for the next little while before dinner. I think you'll love it."

Okay, I felt a little bit better. "I will."

With that, she released me and walked toward the woman who was hovering a few feet away. It was clear she wanted to let us finish our conversation but still needed help.

Irritation buzzed inside me, but I quickly squashed it. Cari couldn't help it that I made the impulsive move to drive to Devil Springs without warning her I was coming. Or that she had a job she needed to do.

It would be selfish to expect her to drop everything and close her store to show me around. Even though a tiny part of me wished that she had done exactly that.

Those weren't fair thoughts. They weren't fair to Cari, and they weren't fair to me. I'd made the choice to spring a surprise visit on her. I couldn't be upset at how things were going now.

I closed my fist around the keys and walked out of the grocery store.

I would have plenty of time to catch up with Cari tonight.

Just because it wouldn't be like old times didn't mean that it wouldn't be great.

Chapter Two

I found the cottage that Cari described with no issues. From the outside, it was small and charming, but once I was inside, I discovered it was much larger than it looked.

I gave myself a quick tour of the house, checking out the kitchen and living room before I headed upstairs to the bedrooms.

The biggest bedroom was bright yet soothing, done in shades of white, light grey, lavender, and light blue. The effect was nearly spa-like.

The bathroom was beautiful, too.

Damn, I wondered if Cari was planning on keeping this place because I loved it. I wanted to move in permanently. Though I'd saved enough for a down payment on a house, I was still renting an apartment in Tennessee because buying a home seemed like a huge commitment. One I wasn't ready for.

I might not want the headaches that came with owning a home, but this one just might be worth it.

I dumped my suitcase in the closet and headed back out the door. The cottage was right downtown, so I didn't bother with my car.

Instead, I walked toward the square, checking out all the shops and other businesses. I saw the sign for the mayor's office across the way but avoided it. While I'd spoken to Daniel on video chat, I didn't want to drop in on him and get a cool reception as I had with Cari.

I mulled over Cari's behavior as I looked around. Her smiles were sincere, so she was happy to see me.

But there was a reserve there, as though she wasn't sure she wanted me here.

It caused an uncomfortable tingle on the back of my neck.

I joked with Cari that it was my "lizard brain" working, but I'd never told her that my intuition was never wrong. Or that I could always tell when people were lying to me.

I smelled coffee as I approached another storefront and realized it was a bakery. A latte and a treat might do the trick to soothe that nagging sensation.

I opened the door and entered, surprised by how many people were inside. For such a small town, there seemed to be people everywhere.

As soon as the door shut behind me, I was reminded of the downside of small towns. Almost as one, everyone in the bakery turned to stare at me.

Yep, everyone knew everyone, which means they all knew I wasn't from around here. No one was scowling, but everyone seemed to be watching me intently. Especially the man who sat in the back corner at a two-top table.

He was very pretty, with golden hair and eyes, but the way he held himself gave me pause. As though he were poised for...something.

Huh. Handsome or not, the tingling on the nape of my neck made my decision for me. I wasn't going anywhere near him.

I waited in line, eyeballing the display case that was filled with cookies, cupcakes, scones, pies, cakes, and even homemade breads. Oh my God. This place was a dream.

I hadn't decided on anything but the latte I wanted by the time I reached the front of the line. I smiled at the tiny woman standing on the other side of the counter. She wore a white t-shirt under an apron the color of pistachios. Her name was embroidered across the front of the apron. Marjorie. I liked the old-fashioned name. It fit the atmosphere of this place.

"Hi, what can I get for you?"

Wow, I hadn't expected that husky, smoky voice to come from such a tiny woman.

I smiled at her. "I'm not sure. Everything looks delicious."

She grinned back at me, her bright eyes twinkling. "I can promise you it is. I baked most of it."

"Well, based on the way all this looks, you must be very good at it."

Marjorie laughed. "Thank you, but why don't you wait to say that until after you've tried something."

I leaned on the counter. "Well, I know I want a caramel macchiato. But which of the treats would you recommend?"

Her eyes narrowed and she pursed her lips as she studied me. "Hmmm. There are two or three things I think you would like. Want to try them all or pick just one?"

"Hit me with 'em all," I said, digging my wallet out of my purse.

Marjorie smiled even wider, looking absolutely delighted by my choices. After she told the other woman behind the counter to make my coffee, she moved to the display case.

"So, what brings you to Devil Springs?" she asked.

"I'm visiting a friend."

"Oh, really. Who are you visiting?"

"Cari Shelton. She inherited the grocery store down the street."

Marjorie paused for a moment, tilting her head as she studied me. "Are you Sela?"

Warmth permeated my chest. Cari had told this woman about me? Maybe I was exaggerating her hesitancy earlier.

"Yes, I'm Sela Harper."

Marjorie laughed. "Oh, I was hoping I'd get to meet you! Cari has mentioned you quite a bit since she came to town."

"You should only believe half of what she says," I replied.

"Why? Is she lying?"

I shook my head. "No, she only knows the half of it."

Marjorie laughed again. The sound was melodious and enthralling.

"I can see she wasn't lying at all," she answered after she finally stopped laughing.

"About what?"

"That you're funny and tend to say what you're thinking. I appreciate both of those qualities."

We were smiling at each other as she slipped a cookie, some kind of brownie, and what looked like a cannoli into the bag.

"How long are you in town for?" Marjorie asked as she brought the bag over to me.

I took the bag and gave her my debit card before I answered.

"I'm not sure. I was originally planning six weeks, but Cari and Daniel are in the honeymoon phase, and I don't want to be a third wheel."

"Six weeks?"

I shrugged. "I have a ton of vacation days saved up and even if I need to go back to work, I can do it remotely, so I thought I'd stay a while."

Marjorie held out my card and I leaned forward to take it.

As I did, I said, "I haven't met Daniel in person yet, but he seems nice."

Marjorie studied me again, her gaze sharp and knowing. "But?"

I bit back a sigh. Yep, she knew I was digging for information.

"I'm just wondering if he really is that nice or if it's the whole new love stuff making him seem that way."

Marjorie grabbed my latte from the other woman behind the counter. "Normally, I don't like to talk about my customers with others, but I can tell that you're asking out of concern for your friend."

At my nod, she continued. "He's one of the best ma—" She stopped and cleared her throat. "One of the best men that I've ever known. He's honest, kind, and works hard."

"Good. That's great." I was both relieved and frightened by her words. If he really was that great, then Cari was never coming home. This move to Devil Springs would be permanent.

"Then why do you look a little sad?"

I shrugged a shoulder. "I've missed her and knowing that she's finally found a great guy, well, that means I'm going to have to keep missing her."

Marjorie cocked her head. "I'm sorry."

"It's okay. I'm happy that she's happy. She deserves it. Even if it means that I don't get to see her as much anymore."

Marjorie smiled at me. "We all deserve a little happiness."

"Thanks for the treats," I said to her, stepping away. I'd been holding up the line with my conversation.

"I hope I see you again before you leave town," she called as I moved away from the counter.

"You will!" I answered after I sipped a truly divine latte.

While I'd originally planned to eat at the bakery, all the tables were full, so I wound my way back outside and headed toward the benches that surrounded the fountain in the middle of town square.

The air was still chilly, but there was a hint of spring in the bright blue sky. It was the perfect day to sit in the sun and enjoy an afternoon with a coffee and treats.

After I settled on the bench, I opened the bag, pulled out the cookie, and took a huge bite. The flavors of cinnamon, vanilla, and butter melted on my tongue, and I had to bite back a moan.

Holy God, this cookie was the best thing I'd ever put in my mouth.

A shadow fell over me and I glanced up to see the handsome guy from the bakery standing next to the bench.

"Marjorie's cookies are a gift from the gods," he said.

His voice was low and held a little bit of a rumble. It wasn't quite as sexy as the police chief's voice, but it was nice.

I kept chewing and washed the bite down with a sip of my latte.

The man seemed unfazed by my silence because he continued speaking.

"I'm Leo," he said. "Do you mind if I sit with you for a moment?"

Though the back of my neck wasn't tingling any longer, I was wary. But I was also curious about this guy. Everyone seemed to give him a wide berth when he walked my way.

I scooted over to the edge of the bench, leaving him room to sit down on the other end.

He kept space between us as he sat down and angled his body toward me. His eyes glowed like two gold coins in the sunlight.

"Is this your first visit to Devil Springs?" he asked.

"Yes," I answered. "And I'm guessing y'all don't get a lot of visitors."

He chuckled, leaning back against the bench. "We don't. New faces are rare around here."

I sipped my latte and took a moment to study him.

"Are you going to tell me your name?" he asked. He didn't seem uncomfortable with my silence at all.

"I'm not sure," I answered.

Leo chuckled again. "I think you're going to fit right in here at Devil Springs."

"Why do you say that?"

"You're curious but also guarded. Which describes half the inhabitants of this town."

I had to smile. "I'm a big believer in listening to my intuition."

"What does your intuition say about me?"

"That I should keep an eye on you."

He shrugged. "You're not completely wrong."

Before I could ask him what he meant by that, a tall, hulking figure caught my attention.

I turned my head and watched as Chief Kent stomped toward us, his expression murderous.

I glanced around, just to be sure it was me that he was boring holes into with his eyes. Leo and I were the only ones in the area.

I turned to ask Leo if the police chief often marched around town with a scowl on his face, but his side of the bench was empty.

Huh. Weird.

I didn't have time to continue looking for him when Garrett crashed to a halt in front of me.

"What are you doing?" he asked. Actually, it was almost a growl.

Why the heck was he so pissed off?

I got to my feet, refusing to sit on the bench while he loomed over me like a dark cloud.

"I was talking to Leo before you scared him off."

I didn't think it was possible, but his scowl intensified. "You need to avoid him."

He stood too close to me, but I wasn't about to step back. With him, I could guarantee that he would see it as me backing down. No way would I give him the satisfaction.

"Excuse me?" I asked, crossing my arms over my chest.

Shit, I hadn't thought this through. I had a cup of coffee in one hand and a bag of treats in the other. Intimidating, I was not.

I had to regain the upper hand here. Quickly.

"You do not get to tell me who I can speak to. If I want to talk to

Leo or the man on the moon, I can!"

A muscle worked in Garrett's jaw as he stared down at me. His aquamarine eyes glittered with menace.

Maybe I was a freak, but his anger was turning me on. He looked like he wanted to throw me over his knee and spank my ass.

"Leo likes to stir up shit and then step back and watch when it hits the fan. He won't hesitate to throw you under the bus. Just ask your friend, Cari, about what he did to her."

My defiance drained away. "He did something to Cari?"

"He did."

"What—"

"I'm not going to tell you because you won't believe me. Ask your friend."

Annoyance spiked inside me. "That's convenient. He did something bad but you're not going to tell me because I won't believe you. Sounds like a cop out to me."

I bit my bottom lip after I said it because I just realized I told the police chief he was "copping out."

As far as puns went, that was pretty good.

"You've already decided you don't like me," he shot back.

I stiffened, my shoulders going back.

"I haven't decided how I feel about you yet. Despite your assumptions, I like to get to know people a little better before I decide how I feel about them. It sounds like you're the one who doesn't like me."

Those hot blue-green eyes filled my vision as he leaned toward me.

"You have no idea what you're talking about."

Raw heat raced through my body, as if the blood in my veins became molten. He was standing way too close. But I couldn't bring myself to step away. He smelled amazing, like soap, heat, and a darker note of musk.

Forget a tingle on the nape of my neck, my entire body was humming. No, simmering. It wouldn't take much more for the heat to turn to a boil.

Before I could formulate a reply, he turned on his heel and walked away.

And I couldn't tear my gaze away from his backside the entire time.

Chapter Three

After my strange encounters with Leo and Garrett the police chief, I went back to Cari's cottage and took a cool shower. Though it was still nippy out, my body felt too hot, and my skin felt too tight.

The shower calmed me down enough that I realized how tired I was. A quick glance at the clock showed I had plenty of time to take a nap before I had to get ready for dinner.

I stretched out on the bed, groaning at the heavenly feel of the mattress. Dear God, not only was the bedroom gorgeous, the bed was one of the best I'd ever felt.

I set a timer for ninety minutes and let myself melt into the bed. This was going to be the best nap ever.

When the alarm went off an hour and a half later, I was rested but vaguely unsettled, as though I was supposed to do something. The shadowy memory danced on the edges of my mind but never became clear.

Sighing heavily, I sat up and pushed myself off the bed. I had an hour to get ready and drive out to Cari and Daniel's house. According to my navigation app, it would take at least fifteen minutes to drive out there, so I needed to get a move on.

It was strange. The app hadn't worked properly on my way over here, but now that I was in town, I didn't have any problems with it.

I managed to get out the door on time and still look put-together. My hair fell down my back in dark waves and I was wearing a two-piece outfit I'd bought online. I loved the way the coral pink color looked against my skin and the wide-legged pants made my legs look longer than they were. Which was a feat since I was nearly six feet in my shoes. The top was a tank with an elastic hem that didn't quite meet the waist of the pants, leaving a small sliver of my skin exposed. Since it was cold out, I topped the whole thing with a belted cardigan. I finished off the outfit with taupe wedges and slim gold drop earrings.

I adored this outfit because, not only did I feel pretty in it, but it was one of the most comfortable ensembles I owned.

Nerves fluttered in my stomach when I finally pulled into the driveway that led to the house Cari now shared with her new man, Daniel. When the house came into view, I stopped the car. My mouth dropped open as I took in the sight.

It was gorgeous, the house painted a mixture of cream, sage green, and a darker shade of green. Okay, I was beginning to understand the appeal of this town to Cari. This house was exactly the kind of home she'd always wanted. A Craftsman-style house with plenty of windows, and if the chimneys jutting from the roof were any indication, more than one fireplace.

Oh, yes, I could see my bestie falling in love with this house first and the man who owned it second.

I took my foot off the brake and let the car creep forward. The headlights washed over another vehicle parked in front of the garage. A police SUV.

Instinctively, I knew who it belonged to, and my heart rate picked up.

I parked next to the SUV and climbed out, giving the police chief's SUV a cursory glance.

What was he doing here? Did he want to make sure that Cari told me what Leo did? Or that she didn't?

I climbed the porch steps, shivering in the chilly night air. The scent of wood smoke hung around the house. I hoped that meant there was a fire burning inside.

Before I could knock, the door swung open to reveal Daniel, Cari's boyfriend. He was dressed casually in jeans and a sweater, but that sweater appeared to be cashmere.

"Sela!" he greeted me, a wide smile on his face. "I was so glad to hear you'd come to visit."

To my surprise, he was telling the truth. The uncomfortable tingling at the nape of my neck was noticeably absent. He meant what he said. He was glad that I was here.

Some of my nervousness faded.

"I'm glad to be here."

"Come in, come in," he said, stepping back so I could enter.

I sighed when I walked through the door and saw the gorgeous shining wood floors, trim, and the vintage wallpaper on the foyer walls.

"Your home is beautiful, Daniel," I said.

"Thank you. Cari has improved it even more since she moved in. May I take your coat?"

I nodded and untied my cardigan. I had to smile when I saw that Daniel was wearing only a thick pair of socks on his feet instead of shoes. Maybe I'd overdressed for the evening.

"You look very nice," he said.

"Thank you."

"Cari's upstairs, changing clothes. Why don't I pour you a glass of wine and give you the tour while we wait for her to join us?" he asked.

"That sounds delightful."

I looked around, taking in the artwork on the walls and the scent of a wood-burning fireplace.

"Who else is here?" I asked him, even though I already knew the answer.

"Garrett comes for dinner at least once a week. He's joining us tonight. Cari thought it would be a good idea so he can give you some insight into the town as the police chief."

There was a trail of electricity down the back of my neck. He was telling the truth, but not completely.

I followed him back and into a beautiful, rustic kitchen. As he poured me a glass of rosé, I decided to prod him a little about his lie.

"As the mayor, I would have thought you would be able to give me plenty of insight into the town," I said.

Daniel barely blinked, but I could still see the slight hesitation in his hands as he finished pouring my drink.

He didn't answer until he handed me the glass. "Garrett was born here in Devil Springs, and I only moved here a...few years ago. We both know everyone, but he's known them for much longer than I have."

"That makes sense," I said, even though I knew he still wasn't being entirely honest. "Thank you for the wine."

"You're welcome." He turned back toward the hall we'd come through moments before. "Are you ready for the tour? Garrett's camped out in the library in front of the fireplace, so we'll start there."

The butterflies in my stomach returned with a vengeance, but I merely sipped my wine and nodded to Daniel. I had to get over these crazy feelings around the police chief. I planned to be here for over a month. I was going to run into him. It had been less than twenty-four hours, and this was the third time I was going to see him.

And, if I believed that I saw him in the woods on my way into town, this would be our fourth "meeting."

But there was no way he was a werewolf. I mean, sure, he was big and grumbly. And I thought I'd heard him growl earlier in Cari's store but that didn't mean anything. He struck me as the kind of guy who would grunt in place of using words if he felt they were unnecessary.

I took a deep breath and followed Daniel down the hall to the library. He opened the door to reveal a gorgeous library. Literally to die for. Or kill for. The built-in shelves gleamed with rich color and whatever polish had been used on them. The faint scent of lemons mingled with the scent of the wood burning in the fireplace.

Three of the walls were floor-to-ceiling bookshelves, all filled. Garrett was seated on a couch in front of the fire, sipping a beer.

His eyes lifted from the fireplace and pinned me to the floor by the doorway. In the flickering light of the fire and the dim lamplight, he looked like a brooding hero in a romance novel. Or maybe the beast from a fairy tale. Because of the way the lamps were positioned in the corners

25

of the room, most of his body and face were in the shadows, so all that I could truly see was his bulk and the glittering of those piercing eyes.

Daniel flipped the light switch, and another lamp came on, adding to the faint light.

"This is Cari's favorite room," Daniel said, wandering further into the space. "She'll spend all her time in here when she doesn't have to work."

"I can't blame her," I replied.

I ignored the way Garrett was staring at me and walked along one wall full of books. There were collections of poetry, a few classics, and a lot of modern fiction. As I got closer to the corner, more and more romance novels appeared on the shelves and I smiled, knowing that most of them were probably Cari's additions to the library.

"This is a lovely room, Daniel," I said, turning to face him. And Garrett.

Daniel smiled at me, his bright green eyes twinkling. "Thank you. I think it's the main reason that Cari decided to stay here with me."

As though his mention of her name called her forth, my friend appeared in the doorway. "Are you talking about me?"

I sipped my wine as I watched the way Daniel's face lit up when he saw her. I saw glimpses of his adoration of my friend when I spoke with them on video chats, but, in person, it was obvious that he was head over heels in love with her.

He walked over to her, looping an arm around her waist. "I was only telling Sela that you fell in love with my library before you fell in love with me."

She smiled up at him, love shining in her eyes. "Falling for you wasn't too far behind lusting after your library. Or the rest of your house."

Daniel chuckled. "It seemed like forever at the time."

She rolled her eyes, but I could see the flush in her cheek and the sparkle in her eyes. My bestie was just as crazy about this man as he was about her.

"You look pretty."

I jumped and nearly dropped my wineglass at the rumbled words that came close to my left ear. I turned to glare at Garrett, who had somehow managed to get from the couch to standing beside me without me noticing.

How did a guy as huge as him move so quietly?

"What?" I asked, too distracted by the fact that he'd scared me half to death to comprehend what he'd said.

"You look pretty tonight," he repeated.

My stomach clenched at the way he was looking at me. There was no tell-tale tingle on the back of my neck. He was completely sincere.

"Thank you," I replied.

I glanced at his clothes, noting that he wore a nice pair of dark wash jeans and a charcoal Henley that clung to his broad shoulders and wide chest.

"You look nice tonight also."

I couldn't help it. The sincere compliment softened me a little and I had to return it.

His only reply was a grunt and I had to bite back a laugh because that's exactly what I expected from him.

Cari's nickname made sense now. Sheriff Stoic fit him to a T. I wondered if he ever got angry or excited about anything.

His demeanor said no, but I wasn't going to rush to an assumption. No, I was going to watch him and see what happened.

"You look fantastic!" Cari said, distracting me from the unwitting staring contest I was having with Garrett.

I turned to her and smiled. "Being in love agrees with you," I murmured.

Cari hugged me close, her arms wrapping tight around my waist. She was quite a bit shorter than me since she was barefoot, and her head barely came above my breasts, and she squeezed me harder.

I laughed and struggled not to spill my wine. "Are you trying to break one of my ribs?"

She finally released me. "No. I'm giving you the hug I should have given you earlier when you came into the store. I was just so surprised to see you that I stood there like an idiot."

The ache I'd been feeling after her reception earlier vanished. "Not an idiot. I should have warned you I was coming. I forgot how much you dislike surprises."

"You are the best kind of surprise," she argued.

Feeling awkward, I didn't answer with anything other than a shrug.

I was grateful when Daniel interrupted. "I was giving Sela a tour of the house. Could you show her the rest of the place while I finish putting dinner together?"

"Sounds great." Cari looked up at Garrett, who was still standing too close to me. "Why don't you give Daniel a hand?"

Once again, all the big guy did was grunt.

I rolled my lips between my teeth to keep from laughing and Cari's eyes met mine, sparkling with mirth. She knew me well enough to know that I was holding back amusement.

I managed to wait until the men left the room before I laughed. Cari joined me.

"Does he grunt like that often?" I asked her, wiping a tear from beneath my eye.

"Oh, all the time. He barely talks to me except when I cook for him. Then, he asks me to marry him."

I was in the process of drinking more wine when she said it and nearly choked on the liquid. After coughing for a minute, I gasped, "He asked you to marry him?"

Cari couldn't stop giggling, but finally answered, "I think he does it just to annoy Daniel. He doesn't mean it."

I couldn't imagine the big, growly man asking anyone to marry him, much less in a teasing way. It did not compute.

"Garrett is a good guy. He's a little grouchy, but I would be too if I had to deal with a lot of the people in this town the way he does. I'm not sure how Daniel stays in such a good mood all the time because he has to deal with just as many of them."

It was my turn to giggle. "Probably because you're sexing him up all the time."

"Please do not say it like that," Cari replied.

"Boinking his brains out? Playing the gold-medal round of hide the salami?"

She laughed harder and shook her head. "Please stop," she begged.

I relented. "Only if you show me the rest of this gorgeous house."

We talked and laughed, catching up as Cari showed me around the bottom floor of the house. The living room was beautiful, full of antiques and artwork.

But the media room was clearly the real heart of the house. The furniture there was slouchy and comfortable. Movie posters decorated the walls and there was a bar in one corner.

While Daniel had a lovely home and had decorated it well, this room told me that he wasn't as uptight or straight-laced as he seemed based on his profession and demeanor.

We were coming out of the media room when Daniel stuck his head through a doorway down the hall.

"Dinner's ready."

"Good, I'm starving," Cari said. She turned to me. "Daniel is a very good cook. He baked a loaf of bread yesterday and made a pot roast in the oven this afternoon. You're gonna love it."

I followed her into the dining room, loving the navy wallpaper on the walls and the gleaming cherry table that was set for the four of us.

The table setting was simple, but beautiful. Plain white stoneware was set out. Instead of plates, there were wide, shallow bowls on each placemat.

The enormous pot roast rested in a large serving dish, surrounded by chunks of potatoes, carrots, and onions, all sunk in a rich, dark brown gravy. Slices of bread were arranged on another plate and a butter dish sat next to it.

This wasn't a meal for company. It was a meal for family.

My eyes stung at the thought. Before she moved down here, Cari was my only family. At least of my heart.

My parents were still alive, and I talked to them maybe three times a year. Once on their birthdays and Christmas. Any other communication was with cards and emails, which were few and far between. Cari was the only person I truly loved anymore.

Cari gestured to the chair opposite her, but before I could reach for it, a big hand closed around the back.

"Allow me."

I glanced up at Garrett. Once again, he was way too close. "I got it."

I thought I heard a faint growl, but he opened his mouth and rumbled, "Sit in the damn chair."

I barely refrained from rolling my eyes but stepped to the side so he could pull my chair out for me like the overgrown Neanderthal he was.

Though the words were on the tip of my tongue, I didn't say thank you. I was too irritated for that.

After I was seated, Garrett pulled out the chair next to mine and settled in. My eyes widened when the wood groaned beneath his weight. Suddenly, the image of the grumpy police chief falling on the floor because the chair couldn't hold his weight filled my mind.

Oh, God. I wanted to laugh so badly.

"You okay, Kent?" Daniel asked.

"Yeah. Just hoping I don't end up on the floor because of your prissy furniture."

Cari grinned at me across the table, and I stifled a snort of laughter.

Garrett shifted in his seat, his thigh brushing against mine.

Sparks raced across my leg and up my spine. Goose bumps erupted all over my arms and my nipples peaked inside my bra.

Holy crap. I moved my leg as far away from him as possible, but I could still feel the heat emanating from his body.

I desperately needed more wine, but I couldn't have another glass, or I wouldn't be able to drive back to the cottage in town.

I tried to ignore the man sitting beside me for the rest of the meal, but it was proving to be impossible.

Though the food smelled delicious, I barely tasted it because every single one of my senses was focused on the man beside me.

The tension within me grew tighter and tighter until I could no longer pretend it wasn't there. The longer I was around him, the more I questioned my belief that I'd imagined him in the woods. There was something otherworldly about him. Primal. Animalistic. When I looked at him, I saw a man and an animal looking back at me.

The dining room became quieter as we finished our meal. Daniel and Cari still chatted with each other and tried to bring me or Garrett into the conversation, but it wasn't as easy as it had been earlier.

Irritation filled me. Chief Garrett Kent had ruined the night for me. Just with his mere presence.

The longer I was near him, the longer I smelled him, the more my brain thought about those moments in the woods. And the more convinced I became that I hadn't imagined the entire situation.

The tingling on the back of my neck returned with a vengeance and I knew...I knew...that Garrett Kent was a werewolf.

The same way I knew that the sky was blue. Or that Cari would always reply to my texts first thing in the morning with a smiley face.

The only thing I didn't know is what I would do about it.

Chapter Four

Cari looked at me with concern as we finished the meal.

I offered to help her clear the table while Daniel and Garrett put the leftovers away.

While Cari and I loaded the dishwasher, she kept staring at me.

Finally, I asked, "Why are you looking at me like that?"

"Something's wrong. I can tell. Did Daniel or I say something to upset you?"

I shook my head.

"Then, what is it?"

I glanced over my shoulder at the men. They were busy putting containers in the fridge and wrapping up the leftover bread and banana pudding that Daniel had made for dessert.

"I saw something in the woods on my way into town," I finally said. "Something really weird. At first, I thought it was just my imagination playing tricks on me. That I was tired from the long drive, but now, I'm not so sure."

Cari looked over at the men as well. "Let's talk about this in the library, okay?"

I nodded, not wanting to risk Daniel or Garrett overhearing. I mean, the story was pretty crazy. I wasn't sure I should even talk to Cari about it, but I had to tell someone. It was bubbling inside of me like acid and, if I didn't spit it out, it would eat me up from within.

We finished loading the dishwasher and dried our hands before heading out of the kitchen toward the library.

As soon as we were inside, Cari shut the door and turned to me.

"What did you see?"

I rubbed my hands together and paced in front of the fireplace. The flickering flames were comforting.

"Well, I had to pee really bad about ten minutes from town. Only I didn't know it was only ten minutes from town because the stupid GPS kept screwing up. So, I pulled over to the side of the road and decided to go in the woods. After I was done, I heard something moving in the trees, and decided to look around a little. I was worried it was a predator of some kind and I didn't want it to sneak up on me."

My hands started to sweat as I remembered what I'd seen, and I fell silent.

How could I explain this to my friend without sounding like a complete nutjob?

"What was it?" Cari asked.

I sucked in a deep breath. It was now or never.

"It was a huge wolf. I don't mean, big for a wolf. I mean big for any animal. It was the size of a black bear. But that's not even the weirdest part."

I rubbed my hands down the sides of my legs, trying to calm myself.

"A giant wolf the size of a bear isn't the weirdest part?" she asked.

If I'd been calmer, I would have noticed the tone of her voice, and the fact that she didn't sound surprised at all.

Instead, I plowed on. "I know it sounds insane but while I was standing there watching this wolf, it-it…"

When I stopped speaking, Cari came closer, taking one of my hands in hers. But I still couldn't look at her.

"It what?" she asked, her voice gentle.

"It transformed into a man." I turned toward her, speaking more quickly now. "I know it sounds ridiculous. Or like a delusion, but I swear, Cari, I saw this wolf change into a man. And not just any man, it changed into a man I saw today in town."

"Who?" Cari asked.

"Me."

We both faced the doorway, gasping in surprise.

Garrett stood in the open door with his arms crossed as though he'd been there all along. Neither of us had heard the door open.

"Dammit, Kent."

Daniel appeared behind the police chief and nudged him into the library. I took a giant step back, pulling Cari with me.

"You were out in the woods on the road coming into town?" Daniel asked. He didn't sound scary, just mildly annoyed. "You know that we get humans through here sometimes."

Humans? Did he just say humans like that's not what he was?

I blinked. Oh, my God, what was happening right now?

Garrett growled beneath his breath and this time I knew I wasn't imagining it.

"I was trying to chase down one of the Stadler brothers. He got into Vance Neely's backyard again, dug a huge hole, and crapped everywhere because he was pissed that Vance was dating his ex. I lost the scent trail, and I circled back to my clothes to get dressed and call the sheriff's department about the situation, but I got interrupted."

He and Daniel both looked at me and the hair on the back of my neck stood up.

"So, I didn't just imagine you chasing my car down the highway while you were naked?" I asked.

Cari choked at my words, her eyes wide. "You were naked?" she asked Garrett.

He sighed and a dull flush worked its way from his cheeks to his throat. "I heard her moving around in the brush and then caught her scent. It wasn't familiar, so I planned to bring her into town and have you wipe her mind, Ayres. Only she ran pretty damn fast and I was hampered by the fact that I was, uh—"

"In your birthday suit?" Cari supplied, a laugh bordering on the edge of her voice.

The dull flush became darker.

"But I wasn't too worried when I saw she was heading into town. I figured I'd track her down once I was here, only she was with you, Cari," he continued.

I glanced between the three of them.

"You knew he was a werewolf?" I asked Cari, utterly bewildered.

My friend looked at me and smiled, but it was more rueful than genuine. "Yes. Though I've never seen him in his wolf form."

I gestured to Daniel, my anxiety growing. "And what about you? From what you said earlier, you don't consider yourself human. So, what are you?"

Daniel's green eyes brightened until they were painful to meet. He opened his mouth to answer me, and I saw the flash of fangs.

But it was Cari who spoke.

"Daniel is a vampire," she said quietly. "And he's my mate."

Mate? Based on the way she said it, she didn't mean they were just good friends.

"Did he bite you?" I asked. "Did he brainwash you?"

My voice was rising in hysteria. What the fuck was happening right now?

Cari's face turned bright red. "No, he didn't brainwash me. He can't because of the spell that Uncle Bernie—" She cut herself off then, as though she hadn't meant to say anything.

Spells? What in the hell was going on in this town? Her Uncle Bernie cast spells?

Daniel came further into the room. I shifted to the side, trying to keep space between us, and still keep my grip on Cari.

"Back off!"

He frowned at me but stopped moving.

"Cari, you know something has to be done here. The town can't risk—"

"No, you're not wiping her mind," Cari stated. Her tone was harsh. "She's my best friend. My only true friend in the last ten years. You will not make her forget me."

My heart seized at her words. He could make me forget her?

I clenched my hand tightly around hers and backed myself into the corner, dragging her with me.

"I won't let you do this!" I yelled. "I don't care what in the hell you are, I will fight back, and I won't stop."

Daniel's expression turned pained rather than angry as I expected. But he still wasn't speaking to me. The fucker.

"Cari, please, she knows about us. About what we are. You know that I'm not worried about us, but I can't risk the rest of the people in Devil Springs. I have a responsibility toward their safety."

Before Cari could argue, Garrett came forward, standing next to Daniel. "I'll handle it," he said, his aquamarine eyes locked on mine.

Before I could tell him to fuck off, my friend came to my defense.

"No," Cari stated, her voice loud. "There will be no fucking handling of my best friend." She grabbed Daniel's arm, tugging him to face her. "Do not do to her what you planned to do to me when we met."

The fight drained out of me at her words. I was frozen, unable to move or even blink, as I watched them stare each other down.

Garrett made an impatient noise in his throat. "For fuck's sake, Cari, you know we won't hurt her."

Cari blinked rapidly, obviously trying to hold back tears. "You cannot take her away from me. And you can't take me away from her. I won't let you."

Garrett sighed. He looked disgusted. "Do you honestly think so little of me after your time here?" he asked her.

She shook her head. "No, I think you're a great police chief and a good friend, but I also know that you and Daniel would do anything to protect this town. Even if I didn't like it."

"I swear on my wolf that we won't erase her memory of you," Garrett said. "It's a binding vow. There's always a cost. If I break it, I will lose my shifter abilities."

Cari stared at him in silence, a single tear trickling down her cheek. Then, she turned to Daniel. "I need both of you to promise me that you won't have someone else wipe her memories either. No matter what happens, Sela remembers me and our friendship."

Daniel nodded, wrapping an arm around her waist.

Finally, my paralysis wore off.

"Do I get a say in any of this?" I asked, my voice raw and angry.

They all looked at me and my heartbeat stuttered. Cari looked forlorn and both Daniel and Garrett had an intense light gleaming in their eyes. Fear crawled beneath my skin, searing my veins with ice.

They'd just promised Cari they wouldn't hurt me, but I wasn't sure I could believe them. I shifted on my feet, ready to run even though I had no idea where I would go. I couldn't sit here and wait for them to "handle me," as Garrett so succinctly put it. I needed to get out. To break free.

Before it was too late.

As though he could read my mind, Garrett approached me, his steps slow and measured. His hands were held out at his sides, palms open, as though he wanted to prove to me that he meant no harm.

"Don't come any closer," I demanded.

I hated that my voice was shaking. I was a tough bitch, not some weakling who cowered in fear.

"You get to decide what happens, Sela," he said, his gravelly voice gentle and quiet. "No one is going to make you do anything you don't want to do."

Ha! I'd heard that before. Usually from my parents before they shoved anxiety meds and antidepressants at me because they couldn't stand my behavior any longer.

"Stop. Moving," I said. My throat felt tight as though I was being strangled.

Cari stepped around Garrett and came to me. "It's okay, Sela. I promise. If Garrett and Daniel say they won't harm you, they mean it. Garrett isn't a liar. He's almost terrifying in his honesty. You will be safe with him."

Garrett grunted but didn't say anything else.

Tears welled in my eyes as I looked at her. I'd always trusted Cari with things. But never something this big. I wanted to trust her now, but I could see how much she loved Daniel. She would do whatever it took to protect him.

"Do you swear?" I asked her, my voice wobbling.

"I swear, Sela. I would never, ever hurt you or let someone else hurt you. Never. In my heart, you're my sister. I couldn't love you more if we were blood."

I took a shaky breath. "Okay."

"Now, I'll go get a guest room ready for you—" she started to say, but Garrett interrupted her.

"I'm going to take her home," he said.

There was no prickle at the base of my neck. He was telling the truth. He intended to take me home.

Daniel turned to him. "Kent, she's my responsibility."

"She's mine."

He growled the words, and the low rumble of the sound filled the room.

If I wasn't terrified, I would appreciate the sound. His voice was the stuff romance audiobook dreams were made of.

Daniel and Garrett stared at each other, a silent exchange going on between them.

Finally, Daniel gave a short nod and spoke. "Sela is going with Garrett, Cari."

"But—"

"She'll be safe with him. I promise."

"Daniel, I don't—"

This time it was Garrett who interrupted her. "I'm sure Sela doesn't want to listen to the two of you screw all night."

Cari's face turned bright red, and Daniel slapped his hand over his face.

"Jesus, Kent. What the hell?"

My fear abated a little bit then. If he could tease Cari and Daniel about their sex life, then maybe he wasn't planning to murder me and dump my body in the woods.

There was no explanation for it, but I trusted him.

Either way, I needed to take control here. I would not let them determine what happened with me. That was my decision.

"I'll go with Garrett."

At my words, they all turned to me, their faces incredulous.

"Are you sure, Sela?" Cari asked.

"I'm sure."

"Because you can stay here—"

"Cari, I'll be fine. I'm going home for tonight. We can talk tomorrow morning."

If I wasn't wrong about this, that is.

She nodded. "I'm holding you to that."

Garrett walked over to me and held out his hand. "Let's get your coat and I'll take you home."

I stared at his long, thick fingers for a moment before I put my hand in his. The same spark I'd felt earlier when our thighs brushed at the dinner table returned with a vengeance. All the icy fear clinging to me melted away beneath the force of molten heat.

His eyes locked on mine, and, again, I couldn't look away.

Why couldn't I tear my gaze from his?

Garrett laced our fingers together, tugging me away from the corner. I followed him to the foyer, my hand still wrapped in his. He released me long enough to grab my cardigan and hold it out for me.

Surprised by the gentlemanly gesture, I slipped one arm, then the other, into the sleeves. Cari gave me another hug, squeezing me tightly.

"Let me know when you get there, okay?"

"I will."

Garrett was listening, which meant he now knew he couldn't get rid of me until after we arrived at his house and I called Cari.

I took my purse when Garrett offered it to me.

"We'll talk tomorrow, Kent," Daniel said.

When Garrett grunted in response, I had the same insane urge to laugh.

Then, my hand was once again in Garrett's, and he pulled me through the door and into the night.

Chapter Five

Surprise, surprise, Garrett didn't take me back to town.

No, instead he took several turns on county roads, taking us deeper and deeper into the countryside.

Betrayal knifed through my chest. I thought I could trust him.

Tears welled in my eyes and trickled down my cheeks. I tried to remain silent. I wouldn't give him the satisfaction of seeing me cry before he handled me.

No, when the time came, I would fight like hell. He might be stronger than me. He might be a freaking werewolf, but I wasn't going to give up.

"Where are you taking me?" I asked him.

I hated that my voice sounded full of tears.

Garrett's head turned toward me, the movement sharp. "What's wrong?"

I didn't answer. I only repeated my question. "Where are you taking me?"

When he didn't say anything, I asked, "Are you planning to imprison me somewhere? Maybe have me committed to the hospital?"

Though the interior of the car was dark, I could see his jaw flex. His hands tightened on the steering wheel until it creaked ominously.

"Answer me!"

"No," he growled. "I told you that you would be safe."

"Some might argue a prison cell or padded room would be safe."

He slowed and I saw a driveway to the right. The mailbox at the end read Kent.

"Please tell me you're taking me to your parents' house and not yours."

"It is my parents' house, actually."

I stiffened, whirling to face him. "You are not taking me to your parents' house!"

Garrett chuckled as he turned the wheel, pulling into the driveway. "Don't worry, they're not here."

"That doesn't make it any better, Garrett!"

He glanced at me, his aquamarine eyes glittering.

"What?"

"I like it when you say my name."

A thrill raced down my spine.

Oh, I was not equipped to handle a man like Garrett Kent. Not tonight. Not after the emotional upheaval I'd experienced.

I would never be ready for a man like him. Never.

Everything about him screamed danger. Not just the kind of danger he could pose to my body. He was so intense. So focused. If he directed all of that focus on me...

I shivered at the thought.

He might be quiet, but there was a lot going on beneath the calm surface of his personality.

Garrett parked his vehicle in front of a small ranch style home. The windows were dark and there was only a beat-up truck in the driveway. It was older than I was.

I stopped arguing as he climbed out of the SUV. I shoved my own door open and stepped out of the vehicle, right into Garrett's chest.

I stumbled back against the SUV, but before I could say anything, Garrett grabbed my hand and tugged me away. The door slammed behind me as he towed me along in his wake, heading toward the front porch.

Though I was tall, his legs were longer, and I nearly had to trot to keep up.

Our feet thudded on the wooden stairs and porch as we approached the front door. To my surprise, it was unlocked and swung open under his hand.

"Your parents don't lock their door?"

"No need. I would smell any intruders as soon as I got out of the car."

"Do you lock it when you're inside?"

Garrett pulled me deeper into the house, stopping to lean over and turn on another lamp.

The light revealed a tidy interior. The living room and kitchen were directly in front of us, and a hallway led to the right. It was shrouded in darkness.

The entire house gave the impression of emptiness.

"Where are your parents?" I asked, glancing around. The interior reflected more of a bachelor pad than a family home.

"Probably asleep in their beds in Alaska."

"Oh, are you housesitting?"

Garrett moved over to the fireplace along the left wall and leaned down to add wood to the grate. I watched as he took the time to get a fire going.

When he stood, he finally answered.

"No, this is my place now. I grew up in this house, but my parents decided to retire to Alaska of all places and my sister didn't want it, so they gave it to me on the condition that I handle the taxes and upkeep."

I had no idea how to respond to that.

Wait, yes, I did.

"Take me back to Cari's cottage," I demanded.

"No."

The fire crackled merrily in the hearth as he walked away from me and into the kitchen.

"No?" I asked, following him.

"Yes."

I narrowed my eyes at his back and considered giving him a good kick in the ass. "I'm not staying here."

He took an old kettle from the stove and filled it with water. "It's just for tonight, Sela."

"Why?" I asked.

I moved to the counter separating the kitchen and living area. There was a row of barstools there, so I pulled one out and sat on it.

"I know you'll have questions. And I know you're freaked out. That's not a great combination. No one wants to harm you, but we also can't let you leave town until we figure out how to handle the fact that you witnessed something you shouldn't have. This way, you can be comfortable, ask your questions, and I can be sure you won't sneak out of Devil Springs in the middle of the night."

"You could have accomplished that if you came to Cari's cottage with me. You didn't have to bring me here."

"Not exactly. Here, you don't have a car. You'd have to come into my bedroom in the middle of the night to steal the keys and I would hear you."

"You don't think I could be quiet enough that you wouldn't hear me?"

He chuckled as he pulled two mugs down from a shelf and opened a drawer, pulling out a box of hot cocoa mix.

"No, I don't think you could be that quiet. My hearing is extremely sensitive."

I guessed that was true, considering he was a werewolf. According to the romance novels I liked to read, all of a shifter's senses would be sharper than a human's. I guess that was true.

"Besides, I like the idea of having you here."

There he went again, saying things that left me with no decent response. At least not one that wouldn't lead us down a road I wanted to avoid.

It also told me that the sparks I felt when we touched weren't one-sided. Garrett felt them, too.

I'd been ignoring it all night, and I fully intended to continue ignoring it for as long as possible. I needed answers, not a hot werewolf eye-fucking me.

"Is everyone in Devil Springs a vampire or shifter, like you and Daniel?" I asked him as he poured hot water over the hot cocoa mix.

"All of the citizens are supernatural, yes," he answered. "Not all of them are vampires and shifters."

He finished mixing the hot cocoa, added a small handful of marsh-mallows, and brought the cup over, setting it on the counter in front of me.

His eyes met mine. "But it's considered extremely rude to ask someone what species they are here. Because they're all beings of magic, knowing something like that can give witches and humans power over them because they can determine their weaknesses."

"That makes sense. I'll be sure not to ask."

He nodded. "Good. Any other questions?"

Only about a million.

I sipped my cocoa and watched as he moved over to the other side of the kitchen, took a plate out of the cabinet, and opened an old-fashioned cookie jar. He placed several cookies and even some madeleines on the plate.

My eyes widened when he brought the plate over. The cookies were enormous, just like the ones at the bakery I'd gone to that afternoon.

"Did you buy those?" I asked.

His answer was to grunt.

"Grunts aren't their own language. You're not a troll," I retorted. "Use your words."

I swear, the corners of his mouth tilted up for a split second. Though he didn't show a real smile, his eyes sparkled with mischief.

"Yes, I bought them," he rumbled.

"Does it hurt your throat to talk?" I asked, feeling more like my usual sassy self now that I was getting some sugar in my body.

"No, why?"

"Because half the time, you communicate in grunts. I figured there must be a reason."

Again, his mouth twitched. "If you give me shit, you don't get cookies."

I reached out and snatched one. "Too late. Already got my cookie so I think I'll keep giving you shit."

This time, his smile was full-out. My heart stuttered in my chest. He had dimples. Though he had a beard, they still showed. That smile made him go from rugged and good-looking to insanely handsome. Holy shit.

It was probably a good thing he rarely smiled. With him grinning at me like that, he was a total ladykiller.

"I wondered if Cari exaggerated when she talked about you. I thought she had earlier when we met, but now I'm not so sure."

"What did she tell you?" I asked, a little suspicious. When it came to Cari, she liked to punk me, and it wouldn't surprise me at all if she lied to him just to get one over on me.

"That you were the type of friend who would show up in a helicopter with a team of commandos if you thought she was in trouble. That you were the one who inspired her to start sticking up for herself more."

"I wouldn't know where to get commandos, but I would damn well find out if I thought she needed that kind of help."

He actually laughed. With his deep, rumbly voice, it was like a wash of velvet over my skin.

I had to get this conversation back on track or I was going to do something stupid like walk around this counter and kiss the huge werewolf. Which was a crazy urge in and of itself. I'd never felt this ridiculous attraction to a man I'd just met. This incredible pull that I had to fight to resist.

"Back to my questions," I said, washing down my cookie with cocoa. "Is there anywhere I'm banned from going while I'm here?"

He shook his head. "You're not a prisoner."

"But I can't leave town, right? Isn't that a contradiction?"

"Well, you could wear the bracelet that Cari wore when she realized what Daniel was and we wanted to keep her from leaving. It's spelled to keep you in the boundaries that the warlock or witch specifies."

"Like a magical handcuff?" I asked.

"More like a shock collar for a dog."

I shook my head. "No, thank you."

"The alternative is I lock you in a cell at my jail until Ayres and I figure out what to do with you."

I shivered. That sounded like pure hell. It would be like being trapped.

Garrett frowned at me. "That's an absolute last resort, Sela. No one wants to do that. Not Ayres and not me."

"What if I give you my word that I won't leave without letting any of you know?"

His frown intensified. "I would believe you, but only because a promise carries weight here in Devil Springs. The magic is dense here. If you make a promise or a vow, there is a price if you break it. With you being human, there's no way of telling what the cost would be for you."

"Are you serious?"

"Absolutely. A vow from you works, but I want you to understand the consequences if you don't keep it."

"I fully intend to keep it," I said. "If it means I'm not trapped, I'll do it. I can't be trapped again."

"When were you trapped?" he asked, latching on to that one thing I hadn't meant to say.

I shook my head. I wasn't talking about this with him. "That's extremely personal and I'm not discussing it with you."

He crossed his arms over his chest, cocking his head. The way he was studying me made me shift on the stool. It made me realize that underneath that big, growly exterior was a sharp mind.

"All right. We won't talk about it."

Though he didn't say it, the yet was implied. I had no doubt that he would bring up the topic again later.

"So, how do I make this vow?" I asked, moving right along.

"You have to invoke your name and either vow or swear that you won't leave without speaking to me or Daniel. You must use all of our full names."

"Why?"

"Because names have power. A full name gives someone power over you or allows you to give power to someone else. It's the way of magic. The more specific you are in your spells, the better the magic works. Intention is vital to a spell, but it must be clearly voiced."

I took a deep breath and thought about what I wanted to say. The more specific, the better. Which meant I had to leave room for things out of my control.

"All right. I, Sela Harper, swear not to willingly leave the Devil Springs area without speaking to you, Garrett Kent, or Daniel Ayres."

"Willingly?" he asked.

"That is the only thing I have control over. If I'm injured and must leave for medical attention, that's out of my hands."

"That's a good point. Not something that I thought of."

I was surprised he admitted it.

Before I could say anything else, I yawned, my jaw cracking as I did.

"The rest of your questions can wait. You need rest," Garrett said when my endless yawn finally stopped.

"Sorry, I took a nap earlier. I don't know why I'm so tired."

"Adrenaline crash," he answered. "I'll show you where you'll sleep."

"The cups—"

"I'll clean up. You need rest."

He came around the counter, took my hand, and tugged me to my feet.

I followed him through the living room and down a short hall. He stopped at the end of the hall and opened the door. The room was small, but held a king-size bed, which meant there was very little space to walk around it.

"This is my old room," he said.

That explained the big bed. A guy Garrett's size wouldn't fit on anything smaller than a king mattress.

"I'm right next door if you need me," he continued.

Oh, crap. He was right next door to me. I wasn't going to be able to sleep because I would be thinking about that all freaking night.

"Need a toothbrush?" he asked.

I shook my head. I kept a travel-size one in my purse, along with toothpaste. After years of braces and brushing my teeth after every meal, carrying a toothbrush everywhere was a habit I hadn't broken.

"I'll get you a shirt."

"Why?"

He paused. "To sleep in."

I wasn't about to tell him I usually slept in my panties because that was TMI, so I just nodded.

He disappeared into the door to our left and returned a moment later with a wad of white cotton. When I took it, I realized it had to be his shirt. Even though I was tall, I knew this would swamp me because he was huge.

"Thanks."

His hand touched my arm and I nearly flinched as the heat of the contact shot through me. Why in the hell was I reacting this way to him? And it needed to stop already!

"Try to get some rest. You're safe here."

"I will." I paused. "Which bathroom should I use?" I asked, feeling a little silly for asking, but I needed to know.

"There's one attached to the room."

He stepped into the bedroom, edging around the bed, and opened a door on the other wall. He flipped on the light switch for me, which I appreciated.

"Thanks," I said, yawning again.

Garrett came out of the bedroom, stopping in front of me. The hall was barely lit by the light coming from the bathroom. "Good night, Sela."

He was in my space, so close that I could feel his body heat through my clothes.

"Good night, Garrett."

He stared down at me for a long moment, and I held my breath. I didn't know him at all, but I wondered if he was about to kiss me. Oh, God. What would I do if he kissed me?

Probably something stupid like kiss him back and grab his ass.

"See you in the morning," he finally said.

I nodded and scurried into the bedroom where I was going to sleep, shutting the door behind me. I stopped at the foot of the bed and released a long breath.

I was so attracted to Garrett Kent that it was killing my brain cells. I couldn't get involved with him. I was only here for a month and a half at the most. Getting involved would only lead to heartbreak...my heartbreak.

His heavy footsteps finally moved away from the bedroom door, and I heard him walk back down the hall toward the kitchen.

I needed to get ready for bed and try to fall asleep before he came back. If I wasn't asleep, I wasn't sure what I would do when I heard him go into his own room and get in bed.

I dumped my purse on top of the dresser to my right and dug

around for my little cosmetic bag that held my spare make-up, tooth-brush, and some other odds and ends I might need like Band-Aids and make-up wipes for cleaning up smudges and smears.

Cari always teased me about my obsession with being prepared for anything. My purse was huge because my philosophy was "Better to have it and not need it than to need it and not have it."

Once I cleaned my face and brushed my teeth, I stared at the white t-shirt Garrett had given me. I picked it up, clenching the soft fabric in my fist.

The thought of wearing his clothes to bed made my stomach twist.

It wasn't a good idea for me to sleep only in my underwear with Garrett right next door. The idea felt dangerous. What if he came to check on me in the middle of the night?

I had to stop overthinking this. It was just a damn t-shirt. Not a proposition for sex.

I dropped the tee on the counter and stripped out of my comfy outfit and bra. When I pulled the t-shirt over my head, I could smell Garrett. Crap. I was going to end up sniffing his shirt like a creeper all night long.

The tingle started at the base of my neck before it grew to encompass my entire body.

I tried to ignore the sensation because I wasn't sure how sharp Garrett's senses were. What if he could smell the fact that I was turned on?

I shut off the bathroom light and scurried to the bed. Once I climbed under the covers and stretched out, I bit back a groan. The mattress was incredible. It cradled my body. Weird that all the beds I'd slept in here in Devil Springs were awesome.

My phone buzzed, distracting me from the cloud I was lying on. I picked it up and saw that Cari had messaged me.

Are you ok? You were supposed to text me!

I huffed out a short laugh. Okay? I wasn't sure I'd be okay any time soon, much less tonight. But I hadn't meant to forget to text her.

Sorry. It's been a weird night, so I'm not okay yet. But maybe tomorrow.

The three dots danced as she typed her response.

I know it's a lot. I'm here if you need to talk.

And that right there was why Cari was my best, and really my only, friend. But, even as close as we were, there were some things I couldn't talk to her about.

Not because I didn't trust her, but because I couldn't bring myself to vocalize them. The therapists and medications my parents had pushed on me in my teen years. The things that I sometimes saw when I wasn't focused enough. Scary, thrilling, and even exciting things.

I almost hadn't told her about seeing Garrett in the woods, but I'd followed my instincts.

Because I'd listened to my instincts, I discovered that some of the things I saw were real. I wasn't sure if I was terrified or relieved that the unbelievable events and beings I'd seen over the years were likely real.

I typed out a response to Cari, keeping it short and sweet. I couldn't think too deeply on this tonight or I'd never sleep. I struggled with insomnia on a regular basis, but at the moment, I was tired down to my bones.

I love you. I'll talk to you tomorrow.

Love you, too. Get some rest.

I put my phone back on the nightstand and relaxed into the bed with a sigh. I wasn't going to think about this anymore tonight.

And that was the last thing I remembered.

Chapter Six

The scent of bacon frying woke me up from a dead sleep. I blinked a few times before my eyes focused and I took in the room around me.

With a gasp, I sat straight up in the bed, clutching the blankets to my chest.

Then, I remembered what happened the night before. And where I was.

I collapsed back on the pillow with a sigh. I laid there for a few more minutes, staring at the ceiling, then my stomach growled as the scent of bacon became stronger.

Ten minutes later, I'd taken a short shower, dressed in my clothes from last night, though I had a clean pair of underwear in my bag, and brushed my teeth. I had make-up in my purse, but I didn't feel like messing with it.

Despite my worries, I'd slept better than I had in months last night. As soon as my head hit the pillow, I conked out.

I attributed it to the comfy mattress rather than the ultra-soft t-shirt I wore that smelled like a certain werewolf.

I didn't bother with my shoes as I wandered down the short hall toward the living room. I stopped short at the mouth of the hall when I saw that not only was Garrett making breakfast in the kitchen, he wore nothing but a snug black tank top and loose sweatpants.

Immediately, my mouth began to water, and it had nothing to do with the bacon cooking on the stove.

"Breakfast will be ready soon," Garrett said without looking over at me.

"How did you know I was up?" I asked, walking through the living room to the kitchen.

"I heard the shower."

Oh, wow, so his hearing was really good.

"And smelled you."

And his sense of smell was even better.

"Want some coffee?" he asked.

"Sounds good." I came around the bar, thinking I would get it myself.

At the same time, Garrett turned.

We ended up chest-to-chest, barely touching. Well, more like my chest to his upper abs. He towered over me.

I tilted my head back to look up at him. Barefoot, I was six or seven inches shorter than him. I wasn't used to looking up at men.

Heat boiled off his skin and I wondered if it was because he was a shapeshifter or if it was because he was a big, muscular guy.

"I'll get it," he rumbled.

I swallowed hard because I could feel the vibrations of his words against my breasts. Holy crap, that felt good. I couldn't look away from his eyes, realizing that they were the color of a tropical ocean. Both blue and green and constantly shifting between the two based on the light.

His pupils expanded and his hands came to my hips.

My body jerked at the contact, but all he did was nudge me out of the way so he could get to the cabinet that held the mugs.

My knees were weak, so I made my way around the counter to the bar stool I sat on last night. I managed to get my ass on the seat before my legs gave out, but my thighs were still trembling.

This weird attraction I had to him was only growing stronger and he didn't seem to be as affected as I was. He was attracted to me, yes, but he didn't seem at all tongue-tied when he was close to me. Not like I was. I had to get this under control, or I would end up doing something stupid, like trying to climb him like a tree.

"Cream and sugar?" he asked, his voice still low and growly.

"Yes, please."

I watched as he dropped two spoons of sugar in my coffee and piped up, "One more."

He glanced at me, the corner of his mouth jerking up in that almost smirk that he'd given me last night. But he added another spoonful of sugar and stirred it up.

Instead of milk, he took a carton of half and half out of his fridge, poured a bit in, glancing at me for confirmation.

"Little more," I said, which got me another barely-there smirk and he poured a bit more. "Perfect."

I saw the hint of dimples in his cheeks as he put the half and half away, as though he was amused by me, but they were gone by the time he brought the cup over to me at the counter.

He was already walking away when I took the first sip, but I sighed at how delicious it was. He was handsome, tidy, made great coffee, and he was cooking me breakfast. Other than the facts that he considered grunts as effective communication and he almost never smiled, he was my dream man.

"How are you today?" he asked.

His back was to me as he took the bacon out of the pan and set it on a paper towel to drain, so he didn't see my flinch.

I took another sip of coffee. "I'm okay."

Garrett stopped what he was doing and looked over his shoulder at me, his expression skeptical.

I rolled my eyes and shrugged, cradling the coffee cup with both hands. "Honestly, I've always thought that there was magic in this world, but everyone around me didn't agree, so it's almost a relief to know that I was right."

He seemed satisfied by that answer and went back to what he was doing at the stove.

I drank more coffee, gathering up my courage before I said, "I'm sorry I freaked out on you last night."

Garrett finished beating a bowl of eggs and poured them into the skillet before he turned toward me.

"You have nothing to apologize for," he stated.

"You had to feed me cookies and hot chocolate like a little kid."

He shrugged one shoulder and crossed his massive arms over his chest. I realized that he had a tattoo peeking from beneath the front of his tank top. I'd been so distracted by the buzzing attraction between us that I didn't notice before. And I'd been too far away and already running like hell to check it out when I saw him naked in the woods. I had the immediate urge to discover what he had tattooed on his chest. And if he had tattoos anywhere else.

Then, he proceeded to rock my world by speaking more words than I'd heard him use in the last twenty-four hours.

"You are the bravest person I've ever met. Even supes would have been freaked out if they were cornered by a wolf shifter and a vampire last night. And the fact that you trusted me when it would have been easier to try to run away..." he trailed off, his eyes locked on mine.

Finally, after a few seconds, he continued, his voice rougher than before, "I would never betray your trust. Not now. Not ever."

Heat rushed through my body at his words. He meant every single one. My internal lie detector was humming with agreement.

"Why?" I asked. "You don't know me, and you have a whole town full of people to protect. I could post it all on social media, call government officials, news stations. Everyone I know. Why would you think that I wouldn't do any of those things?"

He grunted, which made me want to laugh, and turned around to stir the eggs in the pan.

"That's not an answer," I teased, drinking more coffee.

"What's not?"

"A grunt."

He glared at me over his shoulder, which should have made me pee my pants, but instead, I continued to poke the bear. Uh, wolf.

"You're a werewolf, not a Neanderthal. You can use actual words. Verbal skills are a sign of intelligence."

He grunted at me again, which only made me laugh.

Garrett finished cooking the eggs and brought the pan to the counter, placing it on a trivet in the center of the countertop. Then, he carried over the bacon and a plate of toast that he must have made before I came out of the bedroom.

Plates, forks, and knives followed, along with a butter dish and grape jelly.

"Thanks for making breakfast," I said, putting some eggs on my plate. "But I still want you to answer my question."

"You're welcome," he said, coming around the counter to sit on the stool next to mine.

Our thighs brushed as he settled on the bar stool, and I tried to pretend that I couldn't feel every little inch of our legs that were touching. He was a big guy. It was probably accidental. I didn't need to make things weird by making a big deal out of an accidental touch of his leg against mine.

"What question?" he asked as he put bacon and eggs on his own plate.

"Why do you trust me?" I repeated, nudging him with my elbow. I lifted a finger before he could answer. "And I want more than a grunt in answer."

One of his dimples made another appearance and his mouth curved into an almost-smile.

"You love Cari. You would never do anything to hurt her. I can tell by the way she talks about you. By how the two of you are together. That's why I trusted you. If you did anything to endanger this town, or her mate, you would be endangering her, which I know you would never, ever do."

Man, he sure was chatty this morning. His words made my chest burn with emotion rather than intense attraction. Because he was right. I would never do anything to hurt Cari.

Then, one of his words hit me. "Mate? Cari said last night that she and Daniel are mates? What does that mean?"

"Shit," Garrett grumbled, rubbing one of his huge hands over his face.

"Like fated mates? Or chosen mates?" I asked, thinking of the romance novels I read on my phone when I couldn't sleep at night.

He lowered his hand enough to look at me over his fingers. "You've heard of fated mates?"

"Only in fiction," I answered. I wasn't about to tell him about the sexy books on the reading app I used.

"Well, that's the best way to describe what they are. As soon as he, uh..." Garrett stopped talking and a dull flush lit his cheekbones.

Was the stoic police chief blushing?

I leaned forward. "As soon as he what?"

Garrett grunted. Again. "You'll have to ask Cari about it. Anyway, they were predestined to be together."

"And Cari's okay with this?" I asked, picking up a piece of bacon and biting into it.

It was crunchy, nearly burnt, just the way I liked it.

He frowned at me. "Yeah. She moved in with him."

That was true. Hell, she'd uprooted her entire life to move down here and be with him, so clearly that was a stupid question.

"Do you have a fated mate?" I asked Garrett. "I mean, shifters in general."

He'd just lifted his coffee mug to his lips when I asked and started choking. He coughed several times and I pounded on his back between his shoulder blades.

"You okay?"

He nodded, still gasping for air.

"Need some water?"

Garrett shook his head and wiped his watering eyes.

Finally, his coughing subsided.

I immediately apologized. "I'm sorry. I'm sure that was a really personal question. You seemed cool talking about Cari and Daniel's situation, so I didn't think you'd mind if I asked you about shifters. You don't have to answer."

Garrett risked another sip of coffee before he answered me. His aquamarine eyes were bright and still watering a bit.

"I'm okay," he said. "And I don't mind answering your questions."

I nibbled on a piece of toast and drank more coffee, waiting for him to answer. When he didn't, I asked, "Well, do shifters have fated mates?"

Another dull flush worked its way over his cheekbones and across

CHASED BY THE ALPHA

his nose. "Yes, I do." He grunted and shook his head. "I mean, I will. And shifters can have fated mates. Sometimes even more than one."

My eyes widened. I wasn't sure which of his statements I was more curious about. He had a mate? Shit, here I was perving all over him and he had someone. And why did that hurt so badly?

"You have a mate?" I asked. "Where is she? She's not going to be pissed I'm here, is she?"

He shook his head. "No, I will have a mate. She's out there. She just doesn't know it yet."

Oh, I had so many questions about that, but, if I was being completely honest with myself, I didn't want to know.

"What about multiple mates? How does that work?"

His face turned even redder. "Well, I've never seen it personally, but sometimes pack males or females end up sharing a fated mate. It's rare and it's never happened here in Devil Springs, so I can't give you much information on that."

I nodded. "Well, now I'm even more curious." I drank the rest of my coffee and pushed my plate away. I couldn't eat any more.

"How do shifters recognize their mates?" I asked him. "Is it on sight? Or something else?"

He cleared his throat, the flush in his cheeks fading away. "Smell. We smell our mates."

I nodded. "That makes sense."

He studied me, his expression serious. "Why?"

"Because animals, and, even on some level, humans rely heavily on scent. It's how predators find prey. How prey know to run before they become dinner. And with humans, our olfactory systems are tied to our memories and emotions. Like how the scent of cinnamon makes me wish for fall. Or when someone wears my ex-boyfriend's cologne it makes me want to gag."

Garrett's eyes narrowed. "Did your ex hurt you?"

I shrugged. "Only my feelings. He was kind of a dick and, coincidentally, he had a tendency to let his actual dick lead him around to other women's beds." Which made me wonder... "Do fated mates cheat? Is that a thing?"

God, I hoped not. Cari deserved better than that.

Garrett growled deep in his chest. I shifted back on my bar stool, worried I'd upset him somehow with my intrusive questions.

"Mates do not fuck others. Not only is it considered dishonorable, but it would cause them physical pain to be with another."

"Yikes. Okay, that's hardcore. I mean, it's awesome that cheating isn't a thing between mates, but that it would hurt them physically is another level."

Garrett shrugged. "Once you find your mate, you want no other. Only their scent, their body, is what you crave."

I bit back a lusty sigh because that sounded hot. To be craved by someone. Someone like Garrett, especially.

I shook off the fantasy before I could get too deeply involved because I still wasn't sure if Garrett could smell me when I was aroused or not. I mean, they could in the books, but that didn't mean anything in reality.

And I sure as heck wasn't going to ask him.

"Thanks for making me breakfast," I said, changing the subject. "And answering my questions."

"You're welcome."

I got to my feet and took my plate and his over to the sink. "Since you cooked, I'll clean up. Why don't you get ready to take me back to my car?"

When Garrett didn't move, I glanced at him over my shoulder. He had one thick forearm resting on the countertop as he rested his weight on it. His eyes were on me.

"I can get it," he said.

I waved a free hand at him. "No, you can go get dressed so we can leave. I may be on vacation for the next few weeks, but there are still things I need to do." I paused. "And I'm sure you need to do police chief stuff, too."

The apparition of a smirk spread across his face again. "Police chief stuff?"

"Writing tickets, arresting criminals, and brooding behind your big wooden desk."

"Brooding?"

"Oh, you're definitely a brooder. I mean, you consider grunts an acceptable form of communication."

He shook his head but got to his feet. I could see a dimple peeking out of his beard. Which meant he thought I was funny.

For some reason, the knowledge gave me another flutter in my belly. One even stronger than before.

"I'll be ready to leave in ten," he said, turning to head toward his room.

I leaned over to watch him walk away. Yep, he had a nice butt to go with those huge arms. I'd noticed it yesterday, but the sweatpants really highlighted it.

Once he disappeared from sight, I blew out a breath and fanned myself with my free hand to cool off.

Cari might call him Sheriff Stoic, but the man was four-alarm hot.

Chapter Seven

Thirty minutes later, Garrett pulled into Daniel's driveway and parked next to my sedan.

"What are your plans for today?" he asked.

I shrugged. "I'm not sure."

That damned dimple appeared in his cheek again. "I thought you had stuff to do today."

"I do. I just haven't decided what it is yet."

I got another full smile, his teeth showing behind his beard. "What are your choices?" he asked.

"Why do you want to know? Afraid I'll leave town without telling you?"

"Nope. Now that your feistiness is returning, I figure I need to give people some warning before you show up in town."

I gasped in mock outrage and clutched my chest. "You wound me."

That earned me a chuckle.

My cheeks grew warm at the sound. Dear God, his voice, sexy as it was, his laugh was something else completely.

"Well, maybe I'll see you around town," he said.

"Maybe."

Garrett pointed to the front of Daniel's house, and I saw Cari standing on the porch, her arms wrapped around her body due to the cold.

"I think someone wants to talk to you," he rumbled.

"Yeah." I took a deep breath and let it out slowly.

"Hey," he said, his hand landing on mine.

I glanced down and saw that his huge hand completely engulfed my clenched fist. I'd curled my fingers up without realizing it.

"You and Cari will be fine," he continued.

In his own curt way, he was trying to make me feel better. And he was sincere. I'd dated men who said the same sort of thing when I was upset, but their hearts weren't truly in it. They just didn't want to listen to me vent. They didn't much care that my feelings were hurt or that I was upset about something.

"Thanks," I answer. "For answering my questions and making me breakfast. Also, your mattress is awesome."

"The one in my current room is even better."

My heart gave a quick thud against my sternum and then settled into a quick rhythm. That sounded like an...invitation.

I couldn't formulate a response before there was a sharp knock on my window.

I jumped and yelled, whirling to look out of the car.

Cari stood there, her scowling face all but pressed against the window. "Get out here," she said.

There was a stifled laugh in Garrett's voice when he said, "Maybe you should do what she says. She looks angry."

"Ya think?" I asked him without turning around.

Cari's eyes narrowed further when she heard us talking about her. "I can hear you."

I sighed. "Bye, Sheriff Stoic. Enjoy your brooding today."

"Bye, Sela."

I opened the door and Cari stepped back to let me out. As soon as I shut it behind me, she threw her arms around me.

"I barely slept last night," she said against my shoulder. "I was so worried about you. And that you would think I betrayed you."

"I told you last night that I was fine," I answered, wrapping my arms around her.

"I know, but I was afraid you were just telling me what I wanted to hear."

"When have I ever done that?" I asked with an arched eyebrow.

She released me and stepped back. "Good point. I have to leave for work soon, but you want something to eat? We could run up to the bakery for breakfast and coffee."

"I could have another cup of coffee from the bakery," I answered. "But I already ate. Garrett made me breakfast."

"Garrett?" she asked, her eyes widening before she glanced around me.

Garrett waved and put his SUV in reverse. Cari and I moved away so he could back out and head back down the driveway.

"Yes, Garrett," I finally answered after the SUV was no longer in sight. "Why do you sound surprised?"

"Because he's always mooching meals off of us."

I laughed. "Well, I would too if your husband cooks everything else as well as he did that pot roast last night."

Cari grinned. "What about my cooking?"

"It's good, too," I replied, deadpan.

Cari smacked my arm. "I make good food!"

"You do," I agreed. "But Daniel's is better."

Cari made an outraged sound. "Take it back."

"Nope."

She chest bumped me playfully. "Take it back."

"I can't. You know I don't like to lie."

The corners of her mouth tugged up, but she tried to fight the smile. Finally, she gave up and laughed. "Okay, so you're right. Daniel is a better cook than me, but he's had more time to hone his craft."

Which reminded me...

"How old is Daniel?"

Cari winced. "I don't want to tell you."

"Why?"

"Because you'll give me shit."

I shrugged. "That's my prerogative as your best friend. Just like you give me shit."

"That's true," she sighed.

"So, how old is he?"

"Look, it's too cold out here. Let's go inside so I can finish getting ready and then we can head into town and get some delicious coffee."

She walked away from me, back toward the house, without answering my question. I took off after her, falling in step beside her.

"Don't change the subject," I said. "How old is he?"

She shot me a look as she opened the front door and walked inside. I followed right behind her.

"Cari, tell me!"

"Ugh. Fine. He's a hundred and twenty-five. He'll be a hundred and twenty-six in a few months."

I stopped short. "He's over a century old?" I asked, my brain not wanting to wrap around the number.

She shrugged, crossing her arms over her chest. "Hey, there are humans that are a hundred and twenty-five still alive right now. It's not that big a deal."

"That may be true but they sure as hell don't look like him!"

She laughed. "Yet another good point," she relented. "Come upstairs with me while I finish putting on my make-up. You can tell me what happened after you and Garrett left last night. Did he actually talk to you, or did he just grunt a lot?"

It was my turn to laugh. "Both," I answered. "I'm beginning to tell the difference between his grunts, too. They're nuanced," I joked.

Cari laughed and waved for me to follow her as she headed up the stairs.

I admired the artwork on the walls and the embossed wallpaper in a dark, rich green. This house was gorgeous. And it was Cari's dream home. She had an entire Pinterest board dedicated to Craftsman-style homes and the traditional décor for them.

When we entered her bedroom, I gasped. It was amazing. Even better than anything she'd found for her Pinterest board.

"I know," she said. "It's dreamy, isn't it?"

I took in the huge bed with the tall corner posts, the rich wood of the rest of the furniture, and the small fireplace with a crackling fire burning merrily inside. "Tell me the truth, you're in love with this house and you're biding your time until you can kick Daniel out, aren't you?"

She laughed, but shook her head, a soft look on her face. "I'll admit the house is an incredible bonus, but I'd live with Daniel, even if we were in a tiny studio apartment."

Garrett was right. Cari was happy here with Daniel. She didn't have a problem being his fated mate. It was obvious that she was head-over-heels for him. And from what Garrett said about mates, Daniel would feel the same for her.

"You're happy," I stated.

She smiled at me, that dreamy expression still on her face. "I am."

"I'm glad."

She sniffed and blinked rapidly. "Oh, my God. Enough with the mushy stuff. I don't want to start my day off with tears, even if they're happy ones. Come check out the bathroom while I finish up my make-up."

I oohed and ahhed over her bathroom while she put on mascara and lipstick, checking out the enormous bathtub that looked deep enough for me to soak in it without my knees sticking out of the water. Considering how tall I was, that was a feat.

The glassed-in shower was decadent, all marble and several brushed nickel shower heads set at different heights. Including a rain shower head set in the ceiling.

"Can you drop me at work when we're done?" she asked as we walked back downstairs.

"Sure. You're not taking your car?"

"Daniel will pick me up after work. We usually ride into town together, but I wanted to catch you when you picked up your car."

It felt like old times when she climbed into the passenger seat of my car. We used to go out for coffee or dinner together once a week. We would have lunch at least once a week, too. I'd missed this—seeing her nearly every day. I'd missed her.

We still texted and talked on the phone all the time, but it wasn't the same. I always felt a bit like a third wheel because I could hear Daniel in the background or Cari would text me that they were going to have dinner or about to watch a movie.

As happy as I was that she'd found her person, I worried that she wasn't going to have room for me in her life anymore.

I drove to Bethany's cottage from her house. "I need to change before we go anywhere. Do you have time?"

"No problem."

She followed me inside, typing away on her phone, and I ran upstairs. I found myself taking a little more time and care picking out a pair of snug jeans and an ultra-soft rose sweater that made my skin glow. Just in case I ran into a handsome police chief.

I rolled my eyes at myself as I took five minutes to put on a little bit of make-up. I felt like I was in high school again, trying to look as cute as possible so the guy I liked would notice me.

I wasn't completely sure Garrett had the same level of attraction for me, but a seed of hope had been planted this morning when he mentioned that his bed was even more comfortable than the one in his guest room.

Then again, he might not have meant for it to sound like an invitation.

I'd never been very good at reading signals from men or understanding when a man was flirting with me.

I bounded back downstairs and found Cari standing in the kitchen, scribbling on a piece of paper.

"What are you doing?" I asked.

"I'm making a list of things you'll need while you're in town. Food, toilet paper, stuff like that."

"I planned on going shopping today," I told her. It was one of the possibilities I'd told Garrett I was considering.

"Your best friend owns the local grocery store," she said, shooting me a bland look. "I can gather all this stuff up for you and you can pick it up at the store later." When I opened my mouth, she continued before I could interrupt. "If I forget anything or you want to add something, you can pick it up while you're there."

"I will be paying for my groceries," I said to her, knowing where this was going.

"You get the friends and family discount," she argued.

"Which is?"

"We'll discuss it when you come in to pick stuff up."

I knew what that meant. She wasn't going to charge me. "Cari, I'm staying in your cottage, rent-free. You are going to let me pay for my groceries. You have a business to run."

"We'll talk about it when you come to pick them up," she stated.

Judging by the tone of her voice, that meant the discussion was over.

We'd just have to see about that.

She ripped the piece of paper off the pad and tucked it into her purse before she looked at me.

"You ready to go get a coffee?"

"Yep."

She followed me outside to the car and climbed into the passenger seat. When I started the car, she said, "Remember: just because you know the local police chief doesn't mean you can drive like a bat out of hell. Kent will still give you a ticket if you speed."

I glanced at her before I turned around to head out of the driveway. "Why do you think that?"

"Because he gave me a speeding ticket last month. Which is why Daniel insists on driving me now. Garrett won't give him tickets because he's the mayor."

She did air quotes around "mayor", and I laughed. "Is that the real reason or is it because Daniel follows the traffic laws?"

Cari just rolled her eyes at me, crossing her arms over her chest.

"Don't say I didn't warn you."

I kept the car at five miles per hour above the speed limit and managed to find a parking spot right between Cari's store and the bakery.

Despite the early hour, the downtown square was full of cars.

"Is it always this busy?" I asked Cari as we walked toward the bakery.

"It's actually quieter on the weekends. You'd be surprised how many of the residents here own businesses and work jobs just like everyone else. They like to spend time at home or out in the woods on the weekends."

That made sense. Most of the small towns I'd been to had nice main streets or squares, but there were always several buildings that were empty or that needed renovation. Devil Springs was different. Every storefront had a sign and lights on. It was clear that they made a real effort to stimulate growth in the downtown area.

I breathed in the crisp morning air. The sky was a brilliant light blue, with only one or two wispy clouds floating by. Winter was still holding on, but judging by the buds on the trees, spring was right around the corner.

The scent of coffee and orange wafted down the sidewalk and smacked into me, and it made me wonder...

"Cari, do you think Marjorie uses a spell or something to make the scents from the bakery come out onto the street?"

My friend stopped short and gaped at me. "I never thought of that." I tugged her arm, eager for a giant caramel macchiato like the one I'd had yesterday. "It makes sense, though," she said. "It's a virtual guarantee that customers will come in."

We walked into the bakery and got in line. While we waited, the scent of orange and cranberry intensified. I may have just had breakfast, but I needed whatever smelled so delicious. It was a moral imperative.

I glanced around while we waited and spotted Leo at the back corner table, drinking a cup of coffee and eating what looked like a scone. He lifted his chin at me.

I waved but seeing him reminded me of what Garrett said. He'd done something to my friend, but I wasn't sure what.

"Who are you waving at?" Cari asked, glancing around.

"Leo," I answered. "He's sitting in the back corner."

Cari frowned and looked over at Leo, who gave her the same chin lift. She rolled her eyes but copied his motion. He grinned at her, his face becoming much more handsome.

Before I could ask her about what Garrett said, we were at the front of the line.

"Back again!" Marjorie exclaimed, clapping her hands. "Did you enjoy your treats yesterday?"

She was looking at me, so I answered. "Yes. They were delicious. I had to come back for more. Like whatever orange cranberry thing I'm smelling."

Marjorie's grin widened. "It's scone day here at the bakery. I always make blueberry and cranberry orange but also seasonal flavors."

"What's the seasonal flavor today?"

"Cinnamon pecan."

That sounded good, but the scent of orange and cranberry was still making my mouth water.

"That sounds nice, but I want the cranberry orange," I said.

"Excellent choice. Caramel macchiato like yesterday?" she asked.

"Make it the largest size you have."

Marjorie turned to Cari. "The usual scone and coffee?"

"Yeah. Thanks."

Marjorie bustled off.

"You must have made a good impression on Marjorie for her to remember what kind of coffee you like," Cari murmured, leaning closer.

"Cool. It's always good to make friends with the owner of the best bakery in town."

"It's the only bakery in town," Cari said, smiling a little.

"Still the best I've ever been to."

"Agreed."

I asked Cari about her favorite things at the bakery, and she told me all about them while Marjorie made our coffee and collected our scones.

I hip checked Cari away from the counter when Marjorie returned and asked us if the bill was together or separate. Cari was a few inches shorter than me, so it was easy to block her from the counter while I paid and stuck a ten-dollar bill in the tip jar next to the register.

"Thanks, Sela!" Marjorie beamed at me, whether it was because of the tip or my little scuffle with Cari, I couldn't be sure.

Cari scowled at me as I grabbed my coffee and treats, but she snatched hers up and followed me to a table by the front windows.

She opened her mouth, probably to give me hell for buying her breakfast, but I steamrolled right over her.

"Garrett said that Leo did something to you right after you came to town and that I shouldn't trust him. But you acknowledged him when I pointed him out. What happened there?"

Cari sighed and took a deep drink of her mocha. "It's a long story," she said when she lowered the cup. "And I'm over it. Mostly."

I opened my bag and broke off a piece of scone, popping it in my mouth. Buttery goodness melted on my tongue, sweet but with the tartness of cranberry and the tang of orange. So freaking good.

"Leo's mom is..." Cari trailed off, opening her own paper bag. "A piece of work. She's not a nice person and she thinks that she should be in charge of Devil Springs."

I cocked my head and she continued, "She wanted Daniel's job. She was running unopposed until Poppy and Garrett took matters into their own hands and started a campaign to write Daniel's name in on the ballots."

"Who's Poppy?" I asked.

"Daniel's assistant. Well, she was the old mayor's assistant and decided she didn't want to work for Leona, so she teamed up with Garrett to get Daniel elected."

I had to grin. "Daniel wasn't even running for mayor, and he got elected anyway?" I asked.

Cari nodded.

I waited while she drank more coffee, but when she didn't expand, I asked, "That doesn't tell me what he did."

"He got wind that his mom was planning to have her goons snatch me in order to blackmail Daniel into resigning, so he got his buddies to come help him kidnap Poppy and me. Well, Poppy wasn't supposed to be there, but Daniel left her in the office with me to protect me."

My eyes widened. "He kidnapped you?" The bite of scone I'd just put in my mouth suddenly tasted dry and thick.

"He didn't hurt me. Or Poppy." she sighed. "Daniel and Garrett hate his guts because they think he should have asked them for help, but I understand why he didn't. He isn't always in control of himself, and he was much worse when he was younger. He didn't think they would listen to him because of his past. And that they would blame him. Either way, he knew I'd still be in danger. So, he did the wrong thing for the right reason."

She took another sip of her mocha. "At least that's the way I look at it."

I mulled over her words. They made sense. Leo clearly had a bad history with Garrett and likely with Daniel. As nice as both males were, they had an air of...inflexibility. If they viewed him as a problem, he would always be a problem, even if he changed.

I suppressed a shiver at the thought. I didn't like the idea that either of them might decide I was a problem. If that ever happened, they would likely never change their opinion of me.

"Do you still blame him?" I asked her.

She shrugged. "Not really. I don't think we'll ever be best buddies but I'm not as angry with him as Daniel and Garrett were. But I'm also not an alpha male who likes to control everything."

I laughed a little at the expression on her face when she said it.

"Like insisting you ride together because you got a speeding ticket?" I asked.

She rolled her eyes and took a huge bite of her scone, but she didn't answer.

While Cari chewed, she eyed me thoughtfully. Then, she asked, "When did you and Garrett talk about Leo? You've been in town for less than twenty-four hours."

I shrugged. "After I left your store yesterday, I came here and got some treats and coffee. I saw him in here and then he came out and sat on a park bench with me. We were having a nice little chat when Garrett spotted him and stormed over. Leo left before he got too close. Then, he warned me away because Leo wasn't a good guy and that he did something to you but wouldn't tell me what. It was infuriating."

Cari nodded. "I see."

"What do you see?" I prodded. I'd always hated that phrase. It was so vague, as though whoever said it wanted to make sure that I didn't see.

She leaned forward, resting her hands and elbows on the table in front of her. "Are you sure you want me to answer that?" she asked.

"Yes! That's why I asked."

A smile tugged at the corners of Cari's mouth. "Well, Garrett isn't just the police chief. He's the alpha of the local werewolf pack." The smile widened into a shit-eating grin. "And I'd say he was staking his claim on you."

It was my turn to roll my eyes. "Staking a claim? Like I'm a piece of property?"

Her eyes sparkled with mirth. "Just like all those books you keep sending me."

"That's fiction, not reality!" I argued. "It may give me tingles to read about it, but I don't want toxic behavior in my life. I've had more than enough of that!"

Cari shushed me. "Calm down, Sela. Garrett's not toxic. Not at all. But he is different from the human men you've dated in the past."

"How?" I asked, feeling a little ragged around the edges.

"I can only tell you what I know about Garrett, which isn't a lot. Only that he may be stern and stoic, but he can be sweet. And he can also be gentle." She shrugged. "He's a good man, and if he's anything like Daniel, he'll make an excellent mate."

Mate? I swallowed hard at the word. Not because it scared me, but because it made excitement bubble in my belly. No, more like anticipation, as though I wanted to be chased by the alpha. And caught.

"I'm not sure I'd want a mate, Cari," I replied. "It sounds like it's supposed to be forever." My throat felt tight as I continued, "And I'm not sure if I'm built for forever."

Cari's eyebrows drew together. "What do you think you're built for?"

I shrugged, fighting to keep my expression and tone light. "I like living my life the way I want to. I like being able to do what I want. When I want." I wave a hand at the rest of the bakery. "Like dropping everything to come here. I didn't have to tell someone I wanted to take a trip. I didn't have to ask them if they wanted to come with me. Hell, one of my previous boyfriends expected me to ask permission to do stuff like this. I hated it. We weren't married. We weren't even living together. Why in the hell would I need to ask him if it was okay for me to take a few weeks to go see a friend? Let him know I was going out of town, yes, that's common courtesy. But to get his approval before making my plans? It's completely ridiculous. I'm a grown woman. I pay my own bills. I don't need someone to run my life."

Cari's lips twitched as she shushed me. "Okay, okay, I get it. You like your independence. I don't blame you. But I don't have to ask Daniel for permission to do stuff. And I doubt that Garrett would expect that of you either. And, if he did, then I wouldn't want you to put up with it."

It was on the tip of my tongue to point out that I drove her into town today because her mate didn't want her driving herself because she'd gotten a speeding ticket recently.

But that felt like a deeply bitchy comment, so I swallowed it down. I hadn't been around them enough to see the ins and outs of their relationship dynamic. For all I knew, Cari liked having more time to spend with her man on the drive to and from town every day. And Cari wasn't me. What she wanted in her relationship could be completely different from what I wanted in mine.

My non-existent relationship. Jesus, maybe that was why I couldn't maintain a relationship. I wasn't willing to ask permission to a man who had no right to tell me what to do anyway.

Wow, I really was on an internal bitch roll this morning. I took a deep breath and focused on letting go of the irritation rising inside me.

A shadow fell over our table, and I glanced up. It was Leo, still holding his coffee cup.

"Good morning, Cari." He looked at me. "You must be Sela."

I frowned at Cari. "Have you told the whole town about me?" I asked her.

She shrugged. "You're my best friend. What do you think?"

"She didn't tell me about you," Leo interrupted. "I've heard it around town."

Judging by the way the patrons around us were looking at him, it must have been because he was eavesdropping. No one seemed to like him all that much.

I thought about what Cari told me, and how he'd done the wrong thing for the right reason. I wondered if he'd been doing that for his entire life. Once you were trapped in that cycle, it was really difficult to get out.

"Good morning, Leo," I answered. "Want to join us?"

I could see Cari's jolt out of the corner of my eye, but I kept my gaze on Leo. Judging by the look of surprise that crossed his face, and vanished just as quickly, he wasn't expecting my invitation.

"Thanks, Sela," he finally answered. "But I don't think I should."

"Maybe next time," I replied.

Two furrows appeared between his brows. "Maybe."

Cari and I watched as he walked out the door and strode off down the street, looking lost in thought.

"What was that?" Cari asked.

"I see the way everyone looks at him. He did the wrong thing for the right reason with you, and it makes me wonder if he's been doing that for a lot longer. If so, he's being ostracized for the wrong reasons. He's probably lonely."

"Every time I think I understand everything about you, you surprise me." Cari sighed. "But you're right. The people here cut him a wide berth because of his past behavior. Thinking back, I wonder how much of it was to prevent his mother's scheming from coming to fruition."

I shrugged. "There ya go. I just think we should try to be nicer to him."

Cari scoffed, but there was a smile on her face. "You never want to be nicer to people."

"Only the people who don't deserve it," I retorted.

She laughed and glanced at her watch. "Okay, I have to finish up and go open the store."

She crammed the rest of her scone in her mouth and washed it down with her mocha latte.

"Come by this afternoon and pick up your groceries," she said.

"Only if you let me pay for them."

"I told you that you can pay but you get the friends and family discount."

I didn't trust her, but I relented because I knew she would stand here and argue half the day if I didn't, and she was already late for work.

"Fine."

Chapter Eight

There was a Devil Springs Police Department SUV parked in the driveway when I pulled up to the cottage. Garrett sat on the front porch, his feet resting on the steps and his elbows on his knees.

He looked so handsome that my heart sped up.

As I approached, he inhaled deeply. Then, he frowned.

"You've been around Leo again?" he asked.

Wow, werewolves really did have good noses.

"He was at the bakery," I answered, stopping just in front of the steps. "He stopped by the table to say hello to Cari and me."

His frown intensified.

Before he could say anything else, I continued, "I asked Cari about what happened, and she told me everything. I understand why you don't like him, but I think he's just misunderstood. I'm not going to treat him like crap just because you aren't crazy about him."

Garrett grunted but that was it.

"Use your words, Garrett. I don't understand Neanderthal."

The mini smirk made an appearance. "Not much to say. I told you my feelings, you feel differently."

I cocked my head and studied him. "You're not mad?"

"Not happy," he agreed. "But you're grown. You make your own choices."

Huh. Not what I was expecting from the alpha of the werewolf pack in Devil Springs. Or the police chief, for that matter.

"What's that look?" he asked, the mini smirk widening to a small smile.

"You don't behave how I expect," I answered.

Garrett got to his feet and came down the steps. "And what did you expect?"

"Some bitching, griping, and repeating that you wanted me to stay away from Leo. Or else. Especially since you're an alpha. Aren't they supposed to be bossy by nature?"

Garrett stopped right in front of me, and I caught a whiff of his scent. God, he smelled so good.

"Oh, I can be bossy when the occasion calls for it," he rumbled.

His words hit me right in the pelvis. The way he was looking at me did, too. Heat raced over my skin as it usually did when he touched me.

"How did you know I'm the alpha?" he asked.

"Cari told me. But you're not as controlling as I expected."

"I can't control what others do. Whether they're my pack or the residents of Devil Springs. They're going to make their own choices. If I got angry every time that happened, I'd be walking around pissed off all the time. It's not worth it."

"Sounds like an extremely reasonable and logical decision," I said.

Was that breathy, husky voice mine?

Garrett grunted in response, which pierced the fog of lust that was surrounding me and made me laugh.

"Why are you here, Sheriff Stoic?" I asked.

He grunted again before he said, "Please don't call me that."

I smirked up at him. "Any time you grunt at me, that's what I'm calling you."

His eyes went bright and hot as he stared down at me and I found myself leaning toward him a little, as though he was a magnet, and I was iron.

"I forgot to get your cell number this morning," he said. "And give you mine."

I had to lighten the mood here before I started trying to shimmy up his body like a monkey.

"Ooohhh, I get the police chief's personal cell phone number," I said, taking a small step back. "I must be special."

Those aquamarine eyes locked on me. "You are."

Shit. A fiery wave of tingles went through my body at his look and his words. Maybe he was as attracted to me as I was to him after all.

He held out his hand. "Phone, please."

I took my phone out of my purse and handed it to him. He started tapping the screen with his massive thumb. When he was done, his phone dinged in his back pocket, and he handed mine back to me. The screen was still open to the text messaging app.

Sela

I had to laugh at the short message. Even in text, he was terse.

"Do you have plans tonight?" he asked.

I glanced up at him, pausing at the heated look he was giving me. "Not really. Why?"

"Want to grab dinner with me?"

I studied him. "As a...date?" I asked. "Or friendly-like."

A flush spread across his cheekbones and my heart started racing again.

"Friendly, but also a date," he rumbled.

"Good answer."

One of his dimples made an appearance in his beard. "You didn't answer though."

"I'd like to have dinner with you," I said. "As a date, as friends, or both."

His real smile spread across his face, making his blue-green eyes sparkle.

"Good. Pick you up at six."

"I know Devil Springs is a small town, but is there a dress code for this date?" I asked.

"Something warm and comfortable," he said. "Pants, boots, and maybe a coat."

"You're not taking me hiking, are you?" I asked. "Because that might be fun at some point, but not when it's dark outside. I can't see well in the dark."

Chapter Ten

Dessert turned out to be a rich chocolate concoction of cake, mousse, and ganache, all topped with dark chocolate shavings and raspberries. It was the best thing I'd ever eaten.

The entire time Garrett and I shared the confection, he stared at me with intense eyes. He watched the spoon disappear into my mouth with unwavering attention.

It was both flattering and unnerving.

After we finished, I insisted on helping him wash the dishes. I was pleased to see his cabin had running water and a small bathroom. I was glad that I didn't have to hide behind a tree to pee.

It was full dark outside as we sat in the chairs around the firepit. I draped the blanket he gave me over my lap, leaning my head on his shoulder.

He'd dragged his chair as close as he possibly could, grumbling about how he needed to put an outdoor couch out here, which made me smile.

Garrett twined his long, thick fingers with mine, his palm rough against my skin. His body heat radiated to me, even though we were barely touching.

As I watched the fire, I asked him questions about his life. His childhood. His job. What it was like to be the alpha of a werewolf pack.

It was his answer to the last question that made me laugh the most.

"I didn't think that pre-school teacher would be a comparison for pack alpha," I giggled.

"I have to watch them like hawks, break up fights over the silliest things, and soothe hurt feelings. What else would you compare it to?"

I shrugged. "I don't know because I've never been an alpha."

I tilted my head back, my cheek rubbing his shoulder, and laughed at the expression on his face.

"It sounds migraine-inducing," I commented.

He looked down at me, his expression soft in the flickering light from the fire. "It's not all bad," he admitted. "But it does cause plenty of headaches."

His free hand came up to brush my hair away from my cheek, then lingered. I shifted closer, unable to help myself. He called to a part of me, deep within, and I couldn't resist the urge to touch him. Or have him touch me.

"Garrett," I whispered.

It was a plea. I needed him. His touch. His lips. Anything.

He growled, low and quiet, before he leaned forward and placed his mouth on mine.

It was a gentle kiss, searching and warm. I sighed into his mouth as I parted my lips.

He took the invitation, sliding his tongue into my mouth. The warmth rising inside me turned into a spear of heat that burst inside my chest, spreading throughout my limbs.

I moaned and tried to turn into him, increase the contact between us. The arm of the chair dug into my ribs, and I ripped my mouth away with a sound of frustration.

Garrett's eyes were hooded and hot as I rose and moved to his chair, clambering into his lap. The chair was wide enough that I could rest my knees on each side of his hips. I knelt over his lap, cupping his face in my hands, and I kissed him again.

He groaned into my mouth and his chest vibrated against my breasts, pricking my nipples. His hands grasped my hips, pulling me down to grind against his erection. I dropped the rest of my weight on him, burrowing as close as I could.

Garrett used his hold on my hips to rock me against his dick, making me moan again. Then, his fingers skated up the back of my jacket, beneath the cropped sweatshirt, until they were touching my bare flesh. The callouses on his hands were rough against my skin and I shivered at the contact.

I thrust my tongue into his mouth, digging my nails into his scalp. Garrett growled against my lips, his hands moving to my sides to cup my ribs. His thumbs grazed the underside of my breasts through my bra before they moved up to roughly stroke my hard nipples.

I gasped, arching into his touch, and rocking against his erection.

Garrett froze beneath me, his huge body tight with tension. Slowly, his hands skimmed down my sides until they rested on my waist, lifting me up an inch until we weren't fully touching any longer.

"What's wrong?" I asked, panting against his lips.

"Sela, I can't," he whispered.

"Can't what?"

"I can't touch you. Not like this."

Icy water wouldn't have been as effective to dampening the heat rising within me. I lifted my head, staring down at him.

"What? Why? Did I do something—"

"No," he snarled. "You didn't do anything. It's me. I can't do this with you. Not yet."

I sat back on his thighs, placing my palms on his shoulders. "Why not?" Then, a disgusting thought overtook me. "Do you have a girl-friend or something?"

His fingers tightened on my waist. "No, I don't."

There was no tingle on my nape, no other telltale sign he was lying. I was still wary, but I believed him.

"If we're both single, why did you stop?" I asked.

"Sela, I like you. A lot. Enough that I'm worried it'll scare you if I act on my instincts."

Warmth spread in my chest again and I relaxed in his hold. "As long as I enjoy those instincts, I think I'd be okay with that."

He shook his head again. "You don't understand. Shifters aren't like human men. If we go further, if I taste you the way I want to—"

I tried to clench my thighs together at his words because my

91

thoughts went straight to him tasting me in places other than my mouth, and he stopped talking. His head fell back against the chair. I moved my hands up to his neck and leaned over him, about to kiss him again.

"Stop," he rasped. "Please."

I froze. He sounded as though he was in pain.

"What are you afraid of, Garrett?" I asked.

His fingers moved to my hips, squeezing them rhythmically. "If I touch you the way I want to. If I eat your pussy and fuck you hard and deep, I'll never be able to let you go."

I shivered in his arms. His words were meant to keep me away from him, but all they did was make my blood heat further.

"Goddammit, Sela," he snarled, rising from the chair, and taking me with him. "You're my mate. If I fuck you, I'll bite you. Mark you. It will tie you to me forever."

His words pierced my fog of arousal. "Mate?"

My legs were shaky when he set me on my feet. I was too confused to process the fact that he'd just lifted me as though I weighed nothing.

Instead, I was focused on his words.

"How can I be your mate?" I asked. "We just met."

His head fell back as he looked at the sky. "I know. That's what I meant when I said shifters are different. We recognize our mates right away." He laughed, a low, growling sound when he looked back down at me. "It's probably a good thing you got away from me in the woods yesterday. When I smelled you, I recognized you instantly as mine. If I'd caught you, I'm not sure I would have been able to stop myself from marking you. And it would have destroyed any chance I had with you."

I shivered for an entirely different reason at his words. He was right. If he'd tackled me and bitten me, I probably never would have forgiven him.

"I never expected my mate to be a human," he admitted, lowering his head so our eyes met.

My body stiffened. "Are you disappointed that I'm human?" I asked, hurt searing through me.

"No," he barked. "Absolutely not. It just makes everything more complicated. I don't care that you're human, but you don't understand shifters. We have humans who've grown up here and have mated with wolves and other shifters. But they understand how it works from a young age. With you..." he trailed off.

"With me what?"

"I don't want to frighten you. That's why I brought you home with me last night and why I asked you to dinner tonight. It soothes my impulses. Otherwise, I'd be stalking you, either in human or wolf form. Being apart from our mates after we recognize them, it's difficult. The wolf wants to be as close to you as possible. He doesn't understand that it will scare you."

I sighed because Garrett was right. I wasn't ready for that. I barely knew him. I was insanely attracted to him. I wanted to get closer to him, to know everything about him. In fact, the soul-deep yearning I felt to do just that put me off balance. I'd never been in so deep so quickly. Usually, I tried to ease my way into relationships slowly, always watching for red flags.

Everything that had happened with my parents ensured that I didn't trust easily.

But in Garrett's case, I wanted to trust him. I wanted to lean on him, to let him in.

That alone made me hesitant. It had been so long since I blindly trusted my intuition that I wasn't sure how to go back to that.

Garrett sensed my change in mood. His hands left my hips, releasing me, and I suddenly felt the chill in the air where I hadn't before.

"I should get you home," he said.

While he packed up the cooler and carried it to the SUV, I folded up his blanket. He took it and put it in the vehicle as well. He put out the fire, leaving the grate on top of the pit to cool, and locked up the cabin.

The drive back to the cottage was quiet. Garrett wrapped his fingers around mine as he drove, but I sensed he was holding himself back.

I had no idea what to say. I wanted to see him again, but I didn't want to make things worse for him. I couldn't imagine what it must be like to hold back instincts that screamed to do something you didn't want to do.

How was I supposed to communicate all that?

I still hadn't formulated an answer to the question by the time we arrived at the cottage. Garrett insisted on opening my door for me and helping me out of the SUV.

His hand still held mine when he walked me up the front steps to the door.

Beneath the shadows of the porch, I couldn't see his face clearly, but I could feel his gaze on my features when he stopped and tilted his head down.

I listened to my heart and rose up on my toes to kiss his cheek. He inhaled deeply, rubbing his jaw against my cheek before I pulled away.

"I know I gave you a lot to think about tonight," he rumbled. "But I'm hoping you'll still see me tomorrow night."

His features were lost in the darkness, but he was tense. I could feel it in his touch. In the very air around us.

"Yes, I'd like to have dinner with you again tomorrow," I answered.

The tightness went out of his body and the shadows around him even seemed to relax.

His hand tightened around mine. "Six o'clock again?" he asked.

"Sounds good. Are we having another picnic?" I asked.

He chuckled, the sound brushing against my skin like a touch. "Did you enjoy it?"

"Yes."

"I'm glad, but I said I'd take you to Sam and Remi's tomorrow night. They have great pizza and Greek food. I think you'll enjoy it."

"Since I love both of those foods, you're probably right. Is it a casual restaurant?" I asked.

"Yes."

"Then, I'll see you at six tomorrow evening."

Garrett's hands released mine and moved up to cup my jaw. As he lowered his head, I clutched his shoulders and stood on my toes again. Our mouths met in a slow, leisurely slide of lips and tongue. I made a sound in the back of my throat and moved closer, wanting to feel his body against mine again.

Garrett deepened the kiss and my hands moved from his shoulders so I could wrap my arms around his neck. His arms slid around my waist, pulling me against his body until we were pressed together.

He was hard and hot against me, a solid slab of muscle from head to toe. I shuddered in his embrace when he growled against my lips. The vibrations shot down my throat, through my chest, and straight between my legs.

The kiss grew frantic until Garrett finally ripped his mouth from mine, his chest heaving. I was panting as well, and I rested my forehead against his shoulder.

"I'm glad you came to town, Sela Harper," he rumbled.

"I am, too," I agreed.

"Now, you need to go inside before I do something I shouldn't."

At the dark tone in his voice, chills broke out on my skin. But not from fear.

His arms tightened around me for a brief moment before he released me.

"We'll talk tomorrow," he said, gently pushing me away.

He waited until I'd unlocked the cottage door and was inside with it secured behind me before I heard his heavy footsteps carry him down the porch steps.

My phone chimed in my purse a few minutes later. I pulled it out and looked at the screen. It was a message from Garrett.

Sweet dreams

If this werewolf was trying to steal my heart, he was going about it the right way.

I was already in deeper than I expected and falling fast.

Chapter Eleven

I was in my comfy clothes, face washed, hair in a messy bun, and drinking a cup of nighttime herbal tea when there was a scratch at my front door.

I frowned, looking back at the door, thinking I was imagining things, until the sound came again.

Setting my cup on the console table in the foyer, I crept up to the front door and peeked out the window beside it. A huge wolf sat in front of the door. It looked straight at me through the window and whined, its tongue hanging out the side of its mouth like an overgrown puppy.

"Garrett?" I asked, thinking the wolf looked familiar.

Its head bobbed up and down, like a nod.

I flipped on the porch light and realized that it really was the wolf I saw in the woods yesterday.

Convinced, I turned the light back off and unlocked the door. As soon as I opened it, the gigantic wolf nosed his way through the door, nudging my bare legs with his cold snout.

I squealed and gently pushed his head away before shutting the door behind him. "Your nose is cold," I said.

After I locked the front door, the wolf parked his enormous ass on the floor right in front of it.

"Is this one of those mating things you were talking about earlier?" I asked.

Again, the wolf's, uh, Garrett's head, bobbed.

"Are you staying the night or just until I go to bed?" I asked.

Garrett's furry head cocked to the side as he studied me, which wasn't an answer.

"Well, either way," I said. "C'mon. I'm going to finish my tea and go to sleep. I've had a long day."

The wolf yipped and followed me as I grabbed my tea and carried it back over to the couch.

Garrett didn't wait for an invite, he just hopped up on the cushions and ambled over before he dropped down next to me, resting his head on my thigh.

I put my hand between his ears, rubbing the soft hair there. Garrett released a deep sigh and relaxed on me. Wow, his head was heavier than I expected.

I drank my tea and went back to the paranormal romance I'd been trying to read before he picked me up for dinner.

By the time I finished my drink, I thought Garrett had fallen asleep, but his eyes popped open when I set down my empty cup. He sat up and hopped off the couch, heading toward the kitchen. He stopped in the doorway and looked over at me.

I grinned and got to my feet. "Ready for bed?" I asked, pausing to cover a yawn with my hand.

Garrett yipped again, which made me laugh. I grabbed my cup and phone and walked past him into the kitchen. His nails clicked on the wood floor as he followed me. I washed out my cup, set it in the drainboard, and filled a glass with water to take upstairs with me.

Garrett followed silently as I went through the house, turning off the lights and checking the locks on the doors and windows. Devil Springs might be a small town, but I wasn't familiar with the area or the people. I intended to be careful.

Garrett's wolf nudged me with his nose again, giving my bare thigh a lick. I assumed he was expressing his approval for my actions, but I couldn't be sure.

That was one bad thing about him remaining in wolf form. I

97

couldn't quite discern what he wanted to communicate. I took it to mean he was staying the night. He had said his wolf would want to be as close to me as possible.

"Let's go to bed," I said.

Garrett trailed me up the stairs and straight into the bedroom. I set my phone and glass on the nightstand and fixed him with a look.

"I'm going into the bathroom alone," I said. "Am I understood?"

The wolf rolled his eyes and moved over to the bed. He jumped up, turned a circle, and curled up into a ball on the opposite side of where I slept last night.

Shaking my head, I went into the bathroom to finish getting ready for bed. When I emerged, the wolf was snoring.

I bit back a laugh as I turned off the bathroom light and moved to close the shades on both of the windows in the bedroom. Garrett was still snoring when I turned off the lamp and climbed into the bed.

I burrowed beneath the covers, trying to get comfortable. As soon as I settled, a heavy, warm weight moved up against my back. Garrett stretched out on his side, his belly against my back, and tucked his nose into the nape of my neck.

Everything inside me relaxed at the contact, as though I'd been waiting all night for this before I could go to sleep.

I snuggled back against Garrett's wolf, and closed my eyes, letting his presence lull me to sleep.

The room was still dark when I woke up, but I was uncomfortably hot. I fought against the weight holding the blanket down until only the sheet covered me. A heavy arm wrapped around my waist, pulling me back into the heat that warmed me when I fell asleep.

The scent surrounding me was familiar and welcome, so I resettled my weight and drifted back to sleep, not registering that the arm around me was smooth rather than furry.

* * *

Weak sunlight was peeking around the shades when I woke up again, this time completely. The heavy arm was still anchored around my waist, but the heat was no longer at my back. My nose was tucked against a warm, hairy chest and my left hand rested on a naked hip.

A naked hip attached to a sleepy, very aroused man.

I blinked, registering that the hard bar poking low into my belly was in fact a big, hard penis.

A low, rumbling growl vibrated against my nose and my memories of the night before returned. My cheeks heated when Garrett's dick twitched against me, and his arm pulled me closer.

"Mornin'."

Oh, God. His voice was deep and raspy from sleep. Combined with the hot scent of his skin and the insistent prod of his dick against me, the sound sent fire swirling through my veins. My thighs tensed, squeezing together as my clit throbbed.

Garrett growled again, his face nudging mine to the side so his lips could trail over my throat to my shoulder. The quick nip of teeth against my skin brought a gasp to my lips and made my hips jerk against his.

He groaned, his hand moving from my back, down to my ass. He rocked against me, rolling his hips until the head of his cock wedged between my thighs.

I gasped again as my clit buzzed with heated pleasure. My hand slid over his naked hip, my nails digging into his skin. Garrett groaned against my neck as my hand skated over his thigh and down.

Just before I wrapped my fingers around his impressive dick, he released my ass and grabbed my hand.

"Sela," he snarled. "If you touch me right now, I don't think I can control myself."

The sleepy, aroused part of me wanted to see exactly what would happen if he lost control, but the wary part that had been burned before knew that he was right. My attraction for him was clouding my judgement. If I wasn't ready to bond, or at the very least, consider him for the long term, I shouldn't be touching him this way.

Still, I pouted a little. "Then, why are you naked in my bed?"

Garrett huffed out a laugh. "Apparently, my wolf was satisfied that he got what he wanted and left in the middle of the night."

"Ah, the ol' blame it on the wolf defense."

He chuckled again. "Hear that one often?"

99

I shrugged, lifting my face so I could see his. "All the time."

I squealed when his hand landed on my ass, stinging through the thin cotton of my pajama shorts and underwear. "Hey!"

Garrett rolled us over until he was on top of me, the flimsy sheet, and my pajamas the only thing between us. Then, he kept on rolling until he was on his feet and heading toward the bathroom. I got an excellent view of his thick thighs and ass, as well as the tattoos that I missed the day I saw him naked in the woods. He had a big piece on his back of a wolf howling at the full moon in the middle of a forest. It was gorgeous and incredibly detailed. I hadn't gotten a good look at the one on his chest because I'd been distracted by other things.

The bathroom door shut behind him, but not before I caught a fleeting glimpse of the cock he'd been poking my belly with earlier.

My eyes widened and I laid on the bed, motionless, for a long moment. Holy cow, everything about Garrett Kent was big.

Fanning myself, I climbed out of the bed and headed downstairs to make coffee. If I stayed in the bedroom, I would end up pouncing on him as soon as he came out of the bathroom. And end up doing something that I might regret.

I was at the kitchen counter, adding cream and sugar to my coffee when two strong arms came around me from behind.

"There's a cup for you under the spout," I told Garrett, gesturing toward the coffee maker.

His bristly jaw brushed my temple before he released me and headed over to get it. I glanced at him and smothered a laugh at the sight of him shirtless, but with a white bath sheet wrapped around his hips. The tattoo on his chest was a tribal design that covered one pectoral. It was a gorgeous piece.

To distract myself from the delicious display of his muscles and tattoos, I sipped my coffee and asked, "Why do you do that?"

"Do what?" he rumbled, adding creamer to his coffee.

"Rub your cheek or jaw on my face and neck. You did it several times yesterday and again this morning."

In the bright morning light, the red that flushed his cheeks and neck was impossible to hide.

I smirked behind my coffee cup. "Is this another one of those were-wolf things?"

He nodded and sighed. "Yeah. We call it scent marking. Shifters have enhanced sense of smell and rubbing my face on yours, or hugging you, leaves traces of my scent all over you. It warns other shifters that you're, uh, intimate with someone. We tend to be—" He rubbed a free hand over his face. "Please don't take this the wrong way, but the best word is territorial. When we're involved with someone, we don't want anyone else messing with them. Or touching them. Or even getting too close."

"All the time?" I asked, more curious than irritated.

"It usually settles down after we end the relationship, or we've been mated for a while."

"How long is a while?"

He drank his coffee, so obviously stalling for time that I had to laugh.

"Just answer me, Garrett. I'm curious, not angry. If we're going to keep seeing each other, I probably need to know what to expect."

"Well, I've never been mated, but typically the mated pairs calm down after five or, uh, ten..." He mumbled something else, but I couldn't understand him.

"Five or ten months?" I asked.

"Uh, years."

I had to laugh. "So, shifters are irrationally possessive for a decade or so? Is it just the males, or the females, too?"

That red flush spread down to his chest, making me laugh harder.

"Males and females," he slurred.

"Thanks for being honest with me, Garrett," I said. "I'd rather you tell me about this stuff rather than blindside me with it when I least expect it."

We drank coffee in silence for a few moments. As my brain came back online, I realized I needed to feed him. A human man Garrett's size would need lots of calories, but Garrett wasn't human. And he ate like a damn horse at breakfast yesterday and at dinner.

I wasn't sure I had enough food in the house to sustain him.

Still, I was going to try.

I moved over to the pantry and pulled out a package of bagels that

Cari picked out for me. I split three and arranged them on a baking sheet. I liked to stick them under the broiler rather than in the toaster.

Garrett leaned his hips against the counter and watched me as I moved around him. I tried not to drool at the sight of a shirtless man with huge biceps drinking coffee in front of my sink.

I unearthed some Canadian bacon and realized I'd need half a package just to feed him. Still, it was better than nothing.

"Are you making me breakfast?" he asked as I continued to dig around in the fridge for cream cheese.

"Yep. You made me breakfast yesterday." I emerged from the fridge with a package of strawberries, cream cheese, and butter. "I thought I'd return the favor."

"You don't have to empty your fridge for me."

I eyeballed him. "I seem to remember you eating five or six scrambled eggs yesterday morning, along with half a pack of bacon, and four pieces of toast. I don't want you to end up hungry before lunch."

He threw his head back and laughed. Not a quiet chuckle or soft laugh as I'd heard from him before, but a full-out belly laugh.

I nearly dropped everything in my hands. I set everything on the counter and put a hand on my hip.

"What's so funny?" I asked him.

"I'm six-foot six in human form, Sela. I'm the size of a small black bear in my wolf form. I burn eight to ten thousand calories a day based on how many times I have to shift. I'm always hungry. I had three granola bars when I got to the station yesterday morning after breakfast."

"How do you afford to eat?" I asked, gaping at him. "Do they even pay police chief's enough to do that?"

His laughter continued. He had to set his cup aside and wipe tears from his eyes.

"I don't have a mortgage or car payment. And the local grocery store owner gives me a law enforcement discount." He glanced at my full fridge and pantry. "Though I don't get all my groceries for five dollars."

"Well, should I put all this back?" I asked. "Or will you eat if I cook for you?"

Garrett pushed off the counter, moving closer. "You want to cook me breakfast?"

I nodded.

His arms came around me, his hands clasped behind my lower back. "Then, cook me whatever you want to eat. If I'm still hungry when I get home, I'll grab something else."

I wanted to argue with him, but I held myself back. I didn't have a lot to feed him. I'd have to make another grocery run today and stock up on eggs, meat, potatoes, and rice. Anything that had lots of protein or carbs.

If I had a chance to make him breakfast tomorrow, I'd go all out then.

"Fine," I relented. "We'll have bagels, fruit, and some Canadian bacon. But I'm still giving you double what I make for myself."

"That's fair," he agreed, his mouth twitching. But he managed to hold back a smile.

Considering how stern and emotionless he'd seemed when I first met him, he was nearly effusive this morning. It seemed that the longer we were together, the less uptight he was around me.

I made us a quick breakfast, toasting the bagels in the oven and smearing them with cream cheese. I also fried the Canadian bacon in a huge skillet I found in the cabinet next to the stove. Whatever we didn't eat, I'd put in the fridge for later.

After we were done, I took a minute to wash the dishes while Garrett was in the bathroom. When I turned around, he was right behind me, his arms looping around my waist again.

"I have to head home and get ready for work," he said, his head tilted down so he could look at me.

"Okay."

"Don't forget, six tonight. I'm picking you up for dinner."

I smiled up at him, leaning against his chest. "I'm looking forward to it."

"Me, too," he answered, his voice so deep that it made my stomach pitch.

I didn't have a chance to say anything else. He lowered his head, his lips pressing mine open for his tongue. I clutched at his shoulders as his tongue danced with mine. My head was light when he released my lips and there was a strange tightness in my chest.

"Can I bring a bag tonight?"

"Are you planning to stay over again?" I asked.

He looked sheepish as he met my gaze. "My wolf will probably insist."

"Well, tell your wolf to chill. He can cuddle with me for a bit, but you need to be human and clothed if you're sleeping in my bed again."

His arms squeezed me so tightly that I squeaked.

"Sorry. I'm glad you understand."

I shrugged. "You're a good snuggler. In wolf or human form."

His mouth curved slightly before he brushed my lips with another light kiss. "I'll miss you today."

Before I could answer, he stepped back, dropped the towel, and shifted. I winced as I heard his bones move and realign, but he seemed fine, as though the process didn't hurt. When he was done, he came forward, shaking his furry head. He licked my thigh and nudged me with his nose before he went to the side door and scratched.

I crouched down in front of him, giving him a hug. "Be safe today. I'll see you tonight."

He lunged forward and licked my cheek, before rubbing his face against mine. Scent marking me, he'd called it earlier.

I stood and opened the door, letting him go out onto the side deck. He darted down the steps and took off in a run down the street, heading in the direction of his home.

I couldn't help myself. I watched until he was out of sight.

Chapter Twelve

I took matters into my own hands when I took a shower after he left. I emerged feeling a lot more relaxed and a lot less horny.

I briefly wondered if Garrett would be able to smell what I'd done, but decided I didn't care. He knew I was horny when he woke up this morning. Until we were both ready to do something about it, I'd have to handle business myself.

I took a few minutes to dry my hair and put a little bit of make-up on my face before I headed out to pick up more groceries.

I didn't consider what would happen when Cari saw everything I was buying.

As soon as I walked in the door, she made a beeline for me.

"Hey! Where were you last night? I dropped by to see if you wanted to grab dinner with Daniel and me, but you didn't answer the door when I knocked. I, uh, asked Daniel to check and see if he could you hear you inside, but he said there weren't any heartbeats in the house."

First of all, Daniel could hear my heartbeat?

Second of all, I wasn't going to lie to my bestie. Even though I wasn't quite ready to tell her what was going on yet.

"Whoa. Daniel can hear heartbeats outside of houses?" I asked.

Cari looked embarrassed. "Yes. He usually doesn't eavesdrop intentionally, but I was worried when you didn't answer my knock. I didn't want to invade your privacy or wake you up if you were finally catching up on some sleep, so I asked him to listen in for a second."

I shook my head in disbelief. I wasn't sure if I was freaked out or impressed at how well the vampire could hear.

"So, where were you?"

"I went to dinner with someone."

She cocked her head to the side, a smile on her face. "With who? Have you already made a friend in town?"

"Uh, Garrett took me out for a campfire picnic."

Her eyes widened. "Garrett? A campfire picnic? Like a date?" She stopped and cleared her throat. "And what exactly is a campfire picnic?"

I shifted, fidgeting with the long sleeves of my top. The day was heating up and the sweatshirt suddenly felt stifling.

"Well, he took me out to some property his family owns near the mountains. He has it set up like a little getaway. A tiny cabin, a firepit with Adirondack chairs, and a picnic table. He cooked us steaks on the fire, and we drank some wine and talked. It was nice."

"How did you end up going to dinner with him?"

I shrugged. "He asked me yesterday morning after I got home from having coffee and scones with you."

"What? Where?"

"He was waiting at the cottage. He wanted to exchange numbers."

"Wait, he came by the cottage after you had breakfast together and he dropped you at my place?"

"Yes," I answered.

"And you're just telling me about this now?"

I shrugged again. "I wasn't sure if it was more of a friends thing or a real date, so I didn't want to make a big deal out of it."

That wasn't quite a lie, but it was as close as I got when it came to Cari.

"And?" she asked. "Was it a friends thing or a real date?"

"Definitely a real date."

Instead of being excited, as I expected, Cari stood in front of me, staring up at me.

"What's wrong?" I asked. "Is there something wrong with him? Crap, please tell me he isn't a closet asshole, because I actually like him."

Cari blinked a few times before she broke from her trance. "Shit. Sorry. I was just shocked. I've never seen Garrett even look twice at any woman in town. And, trust me, they look at him plenty here."

"But he hasn't dated anyone?"

Cari shook her head. "Not as far as I know. Based on some things he and Daniel have said to each other, neither one of them has dated in a long, long time. Years probably."

Okay, her answer settled one of my fears. Garrett wasn't a manwhore.

"You like him?" she asked.

I nodded. "A lot more than I should considering I just met him two days ago."

"Really?" She looked like she was about to clap her hands and jump up and down.

"Chill, Cari. We aren't going steady or anything."

I didn't mention what Garrett said about being mates. I wasn't ready to talk about it with anyone. Not yet. I could ask Garrett questions, but as soon as other people found out, it would be all over town.

And if all the women in town liked to look at Garrett, even if he didn't look back, I would be dealing with some hard feelings and catty comments everywhere I went. I wasn't ready for that. Not yet.

Well, maybe I wouldn't, but that was the one bad thing about small towns. Everyone knew everyone else's business. Gossip was like currency here.

"Is that why you came in this morning?" she asked. "To tell me what was happening."

I bit my lip and winced.

"That's not why?" she asked, sounding offended. "Sela, were you planning to tell me at all?"

"Yeeeees?" I answered, drawing the word out.

She smacked my arm. "I can't believe you were going to keep this a secret from me!"

I rubbed my bicep. "Ow, that hurt."

Cari growled at me, and I nearly told her that she was spending too much time around vampires and shifters, but based on the way she was glaring at me, I'd probably end up with another smack to my arm if I did.

"Sela!"

I sighed. "It's complicated, Cari. I'm only in town for a month, maybe six weeks. I like Garrett so far, but it's only been about forty-two hours since I met him for the first time, not counting the whole naked in the woods thing. I'm not planning to pack up my entire life and move here based on less than two days."

She lost some of her anger than. "You're right. Of course, you're right. I'm just not used to you keeping secrets from me."

"I wasn't keeping a secret," I argued. "I only wanted to have a few days to decide how I felt about the situation before I talked to you about it."

"I understand," she said. "But if you weren't here to tell me about Garrett and your date, why are you here?"

"I need to pick up more food."

"More food?" she asked, gaping at me. "I just gave you four bags—"

She stopped, her mouth snapping shut. Then, the light dawned. I could see it in her face.

"Did he spend the night last night?" she asked, her voice low and serious as hell.

"Uh—"

She didn't wait for me to even attempt to evade the question.

"He did! Holy shit, Sela! Did you—"

"No! We only slept. He showed up in his wolf form and cuddled with me all night. He changed back to his human form this morning and had breakfast with me. He, uh, said this happens sometimes when his wolf really likes someone he's dating. He doesn't have complete control of it."

"He doesn't?" Cari asked. "Wow, that's weird. As the alpha shifter, he has the most control of any of the werewolves in town. He can even control their shifts as well."

He could?

That was another for my list of questions to ask Garrett.

"Anyway," I said, hoping to move on from this subject. "I need some protein rich foods. And all the carbs. Garrett told me this morning he has to eat between eight and ten thousand calories a day."

Cari gaped at me. "That's a lot of food." Her eyebrows lowered. "I need to give him more of a discount on his groceries, then. He buys a lot, but I didn't realize exactly how much he had to eat. I'm pretty sure they don't pay him enough for that."

"Right?" I asked. "That was my first thought, too. How can he afford to feed himself?"

"He probably hunts in his wolf form."

I winced at her words. "I can't talk about that."

Her lips twitched, but Cari dropped the subject.

"All right," she said, clapping her hands. "Well, I can help you figure out some of his favorite foods so you can stock up." Cari paused next to the shopping cart I was pushing. "Does this mean he's coming over again tonight?" she asked.

"Yes, he's coming over tonight after he takes me out to dinner."

"Another campfire picnic?" she asked.

I ignored her sing-song tone. "No, he's taking me to the local restaurant. He didn't tell me what it was called. Just that it was owned by two people named Sam and Remi."

Cari's eyes lit up. "He's taking you there? You're going to love it. The food is ah-may-zing."

"I got to try one of their desserts and some of their sides last night. If the rest of their menu is anything like it, I think you're right."

"Oh, believe me, it's some of the best Greek or Italian food you will ever eat. I'm trying to talk them into bankrolling a sushi restaurant though. Because it gets old only having one place in town to eat besides Marjorie's bakery."

I nodded, stopping in front of the refrigerated shelves that held the meat. "I can't wait to try it then. But, right now, I need help picking out things to feed one hunky police chief. You said you know what some of his favorites are?" I asked.

Cari nodded and collected a few packs of chicken breast, a huge roast beef, and a pack of country pork ribs. "He buys this stuff a lot. I'm not sure how he likes to cook it, but he purchases these most often."

He probably made most of this stuff over the open fire. Except the roast.

"Let's get you some potatoes and rice. Oh, and cheese puffs. I think he buys one of those huge containers every time he comes in for groceries."

I smiled at the image of the huge, stoic police chief snacking on cheese puffs. That I had to see.

"Lead the way," I said.

* * *

I enjoyed my time with Cari. She talked about Daniel. A lot.

I think she was trying to sell me on the idea of mates, so I'd find one in town and stay here.

I didn't tell her about what Garrett said. How he called me his mate. I didn't want to get her hopes up in case it didn't work out.

Once I carried the groceries back to the cottage, cursing the whole way for not driving my car the short distance because the bags were heavy as hell, I decided to explore a bit more of the town. There were several shops on the other side of the square I hadn't visited yet and I was curious.

I smelled coffee and pastries as I passed the bakery, but I decided to hold off. They had a lunch menu and I wanted to try it. I'd be hungry after walking around town, anyway.

As I walked, I thought about Garrett. And his insistence that I was his mate. His fated mate. He said that he hadn't expected me to be human, but that he wasn't disappointed.

I wondered if fated mates were all as happy as Cari and Daniel. Or if they would stay that way. My heart pinched when I thought about Cari being unhappy and stuck in a relationship. Yet another question I needed to ask Garrett. And maybe Daniel. Cari wasn't just my best friend. She was the closest thing I had to a sister. In some ways, I considered her my sister. She was my family. The only one who'd ever understood me and accepted me exactly the way that I was.

"Hello, there."

The warm, sultry voice penetrated my racing thoughts, and I looked up. I'd stopped in front of a shop, standing there for God knows how long.

A short, voluptuous woman stood next to me, her long red hair trailing over her shoulders and back, tiny braids and clips scattered throughout. She wore a deep blue dress that fit snugly on her torso before flowing loosely around her hips and legs. Her bright gold eyes were rimmed with black eye liner, her lips were painted a soft red, and she wore silver earrings that dangled nearly to her shoulders. In fact, she wore quite a bit of jewelry, several necklaces, bracelets, and rings on nearly every finger.

She looked like a witch.

I blinked at the thought. How in the heck would I even know what a witch looked like?

"Are you all right?" she asked.

I realized she expected a response. "Yes. I'm fine. I'm sorry, I was thinking."

She smiled at me. Her skin seemed to glow.

"Why don't you come in for a cup of tea?" she asked.

The items in her window intrigued me now that I was actually looking at them rather than lost in my own thoughts.

"Okay," I agreed.

She opened the door for me with a smile and I entered the store. The scent of rosemary and lavender filled the air. It was fresh and bright.

"I'm Minerva," the woman said as she walked by me toward the counter. As with Cari's store, her sales counter was a heavy, old-fashioned wooden one. But it had a glass display case on top, filled with jewelry, crystals, and small sachets.

"I'm Sela," I replied, taking in her shop. There was a wall of shelves, packed with books to my right. On the left wall, there were scarves, hats, and what appeared to be robes and dresses. There were three large antique tables spread throughout the open space in the center, each stacked with candles, crystals, and other things like tarot cards.

Along the back wall, behind the counter, were clear glass jars on floor-to-ceiling shelves, filled with what appeared to be dried herbs.

"Welcome to my apothecary," Minerva said as she filled an electric kettle with bottled water and turned it on. "I carry nearly everything you would need to cast spells, set wards, or prepare for rituals."

I looked up at her. "That's so interesting. I'm not a witch, but your store is lovely."

Minerva cocked her head, studying me. "You're not a witch?"

I shook my head.

She hummed in the back of her throat and moved to the shelves of glass jars behind her. She plucked several from various spots and brought them over to the counter.

I watched as she added herbs to two delicate teacups.

"What are you putting in the tea?" I asked, coming closer.

"Cinnamon for healing and protection, vanilla for tranquility, cardamom for wisdom, and star anise to release your power." She looked up and a mysterious smile spread across her face. "And I'll add honey for a touch of sweetness, because tea is like life, it shouldn't be bitter."

I stopped on the other side of the counter. "I told you, I'm not a witch."

"I know you believe that," she said, her expression softening. "But it's not true. You have untapped power. I can feel it thrumming around you. It's desperate to be released, but something is holding you back."

I shook my head as she spoke. "I'm not a witch. I'm just in town visiting my friend, Cari."

Another smile spread across Minerva's face. "Oh, so you're Cari's Sela. She talks about you a great deal when I'm in the store picking up my sundries."

Sundries? That was such an antiquated term. How old was Minerva exactly?

"That's what everyone I've met has said."

"Having the love of a dear friend is one of life's greatest blessings," Minerva said, sounding every bit like the witch she appeared to be.

I wanted to ask her to drop the schtick, but Devil Springs wasn't a tourist town. It was a home for supernatural creatures, which meant Minerva was likely the real deal. I didn't want to offend her.

The kettle emitted a belch of steam and Minerva picked it up, pouring the hot water over the herbs. I watched as she took an honest-to-God honey pot and drizzled honey into each cup before giving them a gentle stir with a spoon.

"Please, follow me to the reading room," she said.

Reading room? What was that?

I didn't voice the question because Minerva was already walking through a door, the teacups and saucers, one in each hand.

Still, I was curious, so I walked around the counter and through the door behind it where the witch had disappeared. The hallway held two doors, one directly ahead that was clearly labeled "Storeroom" and another to my left. The wooden sign on the door read "Reading Room."

"Would you mind?" Minerva asked.

I opened the door for her and entered the room. Dark wood wainscoting with intricate carved details caught my attention first. Then, I stared wide-eyed at the wallpaper. The background was dark blue, almost the same color as Minerva's dress, and mythical creatures frolicked across the walls. It was so complex and well-drawn that I wondered if it had been commissioned. A round table sat in the center of the space, topped with a black velvet cloth. Four chairs surrounded the table, set in equal intervals. This room could have been in an interior design magazine for witches.

"Do you like my reading room?" Minerva asked as she set the teacups on the table and closed the door behind me.

"Yes. It's lovely."

Her warm smile made another appearance. "Thank you."

She moved around the room, lighting the candelabras in each corner and the group of pillar candles in varying heights in the center of the table.

"Please, have a seat."

I took the chair opposite of the one Minerva chose and took the teacup and saucer she pushed toward me.

"Please, drink," she said.

When I hesitated, her expression became knowing, and she made a show of sipping her tea as well. "It's perfectly safe. In fact, it should make you feel better."

I lifted the cup, inhaling the spicy scents of the herbs she'd put in the tea and the warmth of the vanilla bean.

I took a testing sip, humming at the flavor that burst over my tongue.

"This is delicious," I said.

Minerva smiled. "Magical teas often are, especially when they contain what we need." She took another sip and then a deep breath. "You say you aren't a witch, Sela, but I'm telling you the truth. I sense power in you. It's suppressed, pushed deep, but it's there."

I opened my mouth to deny her, but she interrupted me.

"Tell me, Sela, do you sense when people are lying to you?"

My mouth snapped shut.

"Do you see things others do not? Feel shifts in the atmosphere around you based on people's emotions and intentions?" She leaned closer. "Did your family insist that you were imagining things? Maybe even seek treatment for your mental health when you insisted that what you sensed was real?"

My throat closed at her questions. Because it was all true. Everything she asked me had happened.

"I—" I stopped trying to speak and swallowed hard, my tight throat now filled with all the things I couldn't bear to say.

"You weren't imagining things, Sela," Minerva continued, her tone gentle. "You aren't ill or odd or anything else they've called you. You merely see the world with a vision that mere humans can't comprehend."

My hands shook and the teacup clattered in the saucer.

"Your power has been bound, whether by your own desires or through trauma, but it's on the verge of breaking free," she continued.

I wanted to tell her to stop. To beg. To scream. But nothing came out of my mouth. I sat and stared at her, the tension inside me coiling tighter and tighter but never snapping.

"I can sense many things about you, Sela, and all of them are good. I believe that your power will emerge when you accept your fate. Whether it's through your own discovery or the discovery of your mate. Your true heart."

"True heart?" I whispered.

"The one that pulls you. The one that you were thinking of when you stopped in front of my store," she answered.

She made it sound so simple when it wasn't.

"I barely know him," I argued.

"But your magic recognized him," she said. "Or else you would not be so consumed with him in such a short time."

"Why are you doing this to me?" I asked. It was a plea rather than a question.

"Because I sense your pain." Her smile was sad. "That is my gift, you see. I divine emotions, magic, and the future. And all three of those are within you and are what drew you here."

"No," I said, shaking my head. "No. Cari drew me here. She's my friend. The closest thing to a sister I've ever had."

"That may be, but humans cannot find this place unless they are meant to. Unless their fate is somehow entwined with the magic here. As yours is. And as is your friend's."

A tremor wracked my body. I jumped to my feet, the tingle that typically hit the nape of my neck was engulfing my entire body. The sensation was so strong that it nearly stung. It was different thought. Not the same sensation as when someone lied to me, but deeper, harsher.

"Why are you doing this to me?" I asked again, tears tracking down my face.

I didn't want to cry. I didn't want to give her that power over me, but I had no control.

Minerva also rose to her feet. "I want to help you, Sela. I know it hurts you to hold back as you have been. You're destined to be here, but you're on the cusp. If you listen to the inner voice created by the humans who didn't understand you, I fear you will make the wrong choice. And it will end in heartbreak for you and for others."

I backed away from her, my back hitting the wall. "Stop. Please, stop. I can't do this."

Minerva lifted both her hands in a gesture of supplication. "I understand. We do not have to, I only wanted you to understand—"

I couldn't listen to any more of her words. They weren't lies. The buzz at the base of my skull was silent. She was telling the truth. Or at least sincerely believed what she was saying.

But I couldn't believe. Not now. Not with my memories threatening to drown me.

I darted for the door, threw it open, and ran as though the hounds of hell were on my heels.

Even as I sprinted out of the store, I knew I couldn't outrun the ghosts of my past.

Chapter Thirteen

I had no idea where I was running, only that I needed to escape. I needed peace. But that was something I rarely found in my life.

My legs carried me out of the square, past the neighborhood that surrounded the main street, and into the woods. I dodged branches and brush, but my clothes caught on a few, forcing me to slow long enough to wrestle free.

Air tore from my lungs, coming in huge pants, as I tried to run faster, to get away from the emotions that were chasing me.

It was useless, though. I had no idea how far I'd gone when I finally collapsed on my knees, breathing hard and fighting the blackness at the edge of my vision.

Sweat poured from me and I fought myself free of the cardigan I was wearing. The cool early spring air did nothing to soothe the heat emanating from me, despite the tank top I wore.

I put my hands on the ground, focusing on grounding myself.

"Trees, grass, the sky, a butterfly, soil," I whispered, panting for breath between each word.

Once I went through five things I could see, I started on things I could touch, letting my fingers wander over them. "A rock, dirt, a blade of grass, a fallen leaf."

My heart was beginning to slow. Just a bit.

Three things I could hear. I closed my eyes, fighting to slow my breath so I could hear something other than my pounding heart.

"The birds singing, the wind in the trees," I started. I strained, trying to listen for anything else. There was a yip in the forest from some animal. "An animal."

My breathing was slowing down, and my chest no longer felt as though it were in a vise.

"Two things I can smell," I whispered. "The earth and woodsmoke."

The only thing left was one thing I could taste.

"Tears."

I lowered my head, letting loose the ragged sob that had been trapped in my chest. I rested on my hands and knees, my fingers fisting the dirt beneath me, and cried.

A twig snapped to my right. My head whipped around, and I saw a hulking form emerge from the bushes. I gasped, scrabbling backward on my hands, until I caught sight of the man's face.

It was Garrett.

He walked toward me, slowly, his hands out, showing me his palms. "It's okay, Sela."

A trembling breath escaped my mouth. "What are you doing here?" I asked.

"Minerva called me. She was worried about you."

I lifted my hands to scrub my face, but stopped when I realized how dirty my palms were. I rubbed my hands together, dislodging dirt and crushed leaves, then I wiped my hands on my leggings.

Garrett crouched in front of me, kneeling over my feet. His hands came out, cupping my cheeks, and his thumbs brushed away the tears that were still clinging to my cheeks.

"What happened?" he asked, his deep rumbly voice so, so gentle.

I sucked in a breath that caught in my chest before I was able to release it.

"I ran into Minerva outside her shop," I whispered. "She offered me tea. Then, she started talking about how I had magic, suppressed magic, and that something was binding it. She asked me all these questions and...and..." A sob tried to rise up again, so I focused on breathing through it.

Garrett's expression was thunderous. "She upset you?"

"I don't think she meant to. I just—" I stopped to clear my throat. "Freaked out on her. I don't blame her, not really. I think she was trying to help. There was just no way for her to know—" I shut my mouth with a click.

"Know what?" Garrett asked.

I shook my head. "I can't...I can't talk about it right now."

He studied me with intense aquamarine eyes, but he didn't press for me to speak.

"Okay, let's go," he said.

His hands moved to my waist, and he rose from his crouch, bringing me to my feet with him.

I grabbed his shoulders because my knees tried to give out. He leaned down to grab my sweater and then looped an arm around my back and another beneath my knees, lifting me into his arms.

"I can walk," I murmured.

"I know."

That was all he said, but he didn't put me down. He carried me back through the woods, but not the way I'd come. He strode out to the right and emerged from the trees on the side of the road, his SUV parked there.

I let him place me in the passenger seat, sitting passively as he buckled me in himself.

I used the bottom edge of my cardigan to wipe the remainder of the tears from my face. When Garrett climbed into the driver's seat, he reached into the console between us, pulling a handful of napkins out.

"Here," he said.

I took them and started wiping my face and nose. "Thanks."

Garrett grunted, back to his stoic self. I glanced over at him and noticed his jaw was flexing, as were his hands on the steering wheel.

He kept driving away from town.

"Where are we going?" I asked him.

"My house."

His answer was terse, but I didn't get the sense he was angry with me. Still, he wasn't the warm, open man who'd eaten breakfast with me this morning.

I blew my nose, trying to figure out what to say. The silence stretching between us was growing more awkward by the moment and I had no idea how to break it.

Garrett turned down a road, driving a short way until he turned into his driveway. I realized why I didn't recognize the route. We'd come to his house from a different direction than we had previously.

He parked his SUV, shutting it off, before he turned toward me. "Stay right there," he ordered.

I sighed, twisting the napkin I held between my hands. I felt... hollow. And fragile. As though even a glancing blow would shatter me into a thousand pieces.

Garrett opened the passenger door, reached a long arm through, and unbuckled my seat belt. Then, he gently lifted me from the car.

I didn't argue when he carried me into his house and settled me on his big, slouchy sofa. The cushions cradled me like a cloud. He took my cardigan from my hand and shook out a blanket that was draped over the back of the couch. It looked just like the blanket I'd used the night before.

He tucked it around me. "Don't move," he said.

I merely nodded, watching as he walked into the kitchen. He filled his tea kettle with water before setting it on the stove to heat. Then, he moved around the kitchen, getting a plate from the cabinet and opening his cookie jar.

He was doing exactly what he had two nights ago when I found out he was a werewolf and freaked out. He was making me hot cocoa and cookies.

I bit back a sigh. It was sweet that he wanted to comfort me the best he could.

A few minutes later, the hot cocoa was done. He brought the cups and plate of cookies over to the couch, setting them on the table to my left. Then, he scooped me up, blanket and all, and settled me on his lap. His back was wedged between the back and the arm of the sofa. He reached out a long arm, snagged a cup, and handed it to me.

"Take a few sips," he commanded.

I did as he asked.

Next, the plate of cookies landed on my lap, but he lifted one of the brookies that he knew I liked and lifted it to my lips.

I took a bite, letting him feed me, but shook my head when he offered me another one.

He set the brookie on the plate.

I sipped the chocolate and felt my body relax against his. Maybe he was onto something with the cookies and hot chocolate.

"Why do you give me sugar when I'm upset?" I asked.

Garrett sipped his own hot chocolate and grunted before he answered, "My mother would do this whenever Poppy or I was upset about something. Or if something bad happened. Hell, even if we got a bad grade on a test. It was her cure-all for emotional upheaval."

A smile graced my lips. "That's really sweet."

"Is it helping?" he asked, his voice gruff.

"Yes," I murmured, sipping from my mug.

He lifted the brookie again and I took another bite. His thumb brushed away a crumb from the corner of my mouth.

"I don't want to upset you again," he said. "But, whenever you're ready to talk about whatever it is that happened today, or in the past, I'm here to listen."

I let my head fall to the side and rest against his chest. "It's not a pretty story," I said, glad that Garrett was using full sentences again.

"I didn't think it would be," he murmured.

"I haven't told anyone else this," I said. "But I can tell when people are lying to me. It's like this annoying tingle or burn on the back of my neck."

Garrett grunted and I smiled a little.

"Don't worry, you haven't lied to me yet that I can tell," I continued.

"I won't lie to you." It sounded like a promise.

"I also...see things," I continued. "Things that I can't explain. When I was younger, I used to tell my parents all about it. There were even a few times I was genuinely afraid of the things I saw. My parents, they're..."

I let my words fall away. Was I really going to tell him this?

Garrett, for his part, just held me, offering me another bite of brookie.

After I swallowed that bite, I started talking again.

"My parents are extremely rational." I laughed. "Actually, that's putting it mildly. They're some of the most close-minded people I've ever met. At first, when I was little, they thought I was just trying to get attention. Then, as I got older, they thought something was wrong with me. They took me to therapists, psychiatrists. I started taking antidepressants when I was fourteen. Things only got worse from there because, instead of keeping my mouth shut, I got louder. Angrier. I couldn't understand why no one would just fucking listen. Why no one would believe me when I told them that the things I saw, the things I heard, were real."

I took a shaky breath. The next part of my story was much more difficult to tell.

"When I was seventeen, I was so angry and rebellious and insistent, that my parents threatened to put me in a psychiatric facility. They ended up settling on boarding school. It was the worst year of my life. My senior year and I was surrounded by people I didn't know and who didn't want to know me."

His hold on me tightened.

"I was still angry and defiant. Then, it was like they just...forgot about me. At first, they called once a week. Then, once every two or three weeks. By the end, in the last two or three months of school, I think they called twice."

Garrett didn't press me when I stopped talking again, lost in my memories.

I took another shaky breath. "I turned eighteen before I graduated, but I stuck out school because I knew I needed my diploma. Once that was done, I came home, packed my stuff, and I left. I worked two jobs for a while, putting myself through junior college. Then, I went to state school on a partial scholarship and using some money my grandmother left me when she died. She tied it up in a trust, so it could only be used for my education or after I turned twenty-five. I didn't mind though. Things were tough until I graduated college, but I was free. That was all that mattered. My parents, they..."

My throat grew tight again and I drank some chocolate to wash away the knot in my throat.

"They tried to keep in touch with me, but I told them that I didn't want to see them anymore." A watery laugh escaped me. "I hate remembering this, but they were relieved. I could feel it, deep in my gut. They didn't want me anymore. Not since they realized I was defective. That was why they sent me away. They were embarrassed that their only daughter was a weirdo."

I curled up into myself. "And then I meet a woman, a complete stranger, who not only knows all of this about me, but she tells me that they were wrong. That I was right. I did see things. I did experience the unexplainable. Because I'm a freaking witch."

A wild laugh escaped me. "A witch! That I have power but that it's bound, either by my intention or my trauma." The last word dripped with disdain. "Trauma is such a mild word for the hell that my childhood was. My parents weren't cruel. Just dismissive. But my life was still so painful because no one listened. And, deep down, I don't think they even cared."

Garrett took the empty cup from my hands and moved the plate off my lap. Then, I was wrapped in the tightest embrace. His hand cradled my head against his chest and the other held me as close as he could.

"I'm so sorry, Sela," he rasped, rocking me gently. "I wish I could go back and save you from that pain."

I tucked my forehead against his neck.

"I'm not sure what's worse," I murmured.

"What?"

"Finally moving on from all of that or knowing that I was right the entire time."

He growled low in his chest, but the vibrations were soothing.

"Can we stay here a while?" I asked, burrowing closer.

"Absolutely."

"Will you hold me while I sleep?"

"Always."

I cuddled closer to him as he stretched out on his back. I was laying slightly to the side, but still on top of him. I wrapped an arm around his waist and buried my face against his shoulder.

His huge hand rubbed my back in a soothing motion, lulling me into sleep.

The tension inside me was fading. I'd told him the worst of my past and he wasn't looking at me like my parents had. Or the one boyfriend I told in college. No, he was holding me like I was precious.

Like he never wanted to let me go.

Chapter Fourteen

I was warm when I woke up, and still cradled against Garrett's chest. He hadn't moved since I passed out.

I laid there, blinking away sleep and listening to the steady thump of his heartbeat. Then, Garrett let loose a loud snore, sounding more like a bear than a man.

I stifled a giggle, but the shaking of my body must have disturbed him, because the next snore was cut short. Garrett growled, rubbing his cheek and nose against my hair.

"You're awake," he rumbled, his voice deeper since he was sleepy.

"I think a bear woke me up," I teased.

"We don't have bears here," he said. He sounded as though he were barely awake.

"I'm sleeping with one," I joked, poking him with my finger in the ribs.

Garrett jerked, reaching down to grab my finger. "Hey."

"Are you ticklish?" I asked.

I evaded his hand and poked him again, making him jump.

"You are!" I cackled with glee.

Then, I attacked. I dug the fingers of both hands into his ribs, moving to straddle his hips so I could get a better angle.

Garrett gasped and tried to grab my hands. But he was trying to be gentle, so he couldn't get a good grip on me.

My fingers skated up and down his ribs, tickling him mercilessly.

He finally gave up trying to grab my hands and pulled me into a bear hug, flipping us over so that I was beneath him on the couch. The air went out of me when I landed with a thump and his fingers encircled my wrists before I could get away, pinning them above my head.

He loomed over me, panting. His jaw worked like he wanted to say something, but nothing came out.

"Use your words," I said, laughing up at him.

"You...you..."

I laughed again, trying to wiggle free. "I can't believe the big, bad wolf is ticklish."

"Sela," he said, my name a warning.

My legs were around his hips, and I tried to bridge and throw him off me, but the couch was too soft for me to get purchase with my feet. Then, I felt it.

His erection pressed against my core, and I gasped.

Garrett groaned, letting his weight rest more heavily against me. "I tried to warn you."

I wrapped my legs around his waist, pulling him closer. His lips hovered a few inches above mine.

"Warn me about what?" I asked, using my legs to pull me up and rub against him.

"That things were going too far."

He groaned again, grinding his hips against mine. Exactly where I needed him.

"Kiss me," I demanded.

"Sela."

I didn't wait for him to deny me again. I lifted my head and nipped his lower lip, tugging it with my teeth.

"I've always wanted to make out with the big, bad wolf," I whispered before I licked the spot I'd just bitten. "I never understood why Little Red Riding Hood ran away."

His eyes on me were so intense that I had to squirm beneath him. A low growl escaped his chest. I tried to wiggle my wrists out of his grip, but he had me pinned.

If I couldn't escape him, then I'd make him come to me. I wrapped my legs tighter around his waist and pulled him into me, until the hard ridge of his cock was right where I needed it.

Garrett stared at me, his eyes taking on a wild gleam. "You don't know what you're asking for," he said.

"I'm asking for you to kiss me, Garrett. Not perform brain surgery."

He kept looking at me for so long that I was ready to give up.

Until he slowly lowered his head, his gaze never leaving mine. When his lips touched mine, I sighed into his mouth. He kissed me with a tenderness that I'd never experienced before.

Warmth shimmered in my belly, spreading throughout my body. I tried to get closer, to increase the contact between us, but Garrett kept the kiss light. He pulled away from me when I arched higher.

"Garrett," I gasped. "Stop teasing me."

"You wanted me to kiss you. You don't get to decide how."

Garrett's lips traveled over my jaw and down my throat. I tilted my head back, eager for his touch.

"So, you're planning on teasing me until I'm crazy?" I asked.

"No, just until I'm satisfied."

His teeth scraped the skin between my neck and shoulder, then he soothed the sting with his tongue.

"And when will that be?" My voice was breathy. Needy.

"When you come for me."

He transferred my wrists to one hand, still keeping them pinned above my head, but I wasn't trying to escape any longer. He was going to stop this ache between my thighs. My entire body was throbbing, and I was so turned on that I doubted it would take much to push me over the edge.

"Can I touch you, Sela? Make you feel good?"

He trailed a long finger down the center of my throat until it stopped just above the low neckline of my tank. My skin erupted in goose bumps at the light caress and the faint scratch of his calluses against my neck.

"Yes," I whispered.

His brilliant blue-green eyes locked on mine for a moment before he looked down where he was touching my chest. His hand moved to my breast, cupping me over the fabric of my top. His thumb slipped over my nipple, the friction of the material between our skin making me gasp again.

My body was heating up from the inside out. I wondered if I would burst into flames before he was done with me.

I sighed in disappointment when his hand moved to my ribs, tracing over each one, down to my waist.

Then, his fingers dipped beneath the hem of my shirt. My stomach contracted as he pushed the cotton up until it was gathered above my breasts. I'd chosen my thin bralette for comfort rather than its prettiness, but my breath still caught in my throat at the way Garrett stared at my breasts.

He tugged one of the cups aside, revealing my nipple, and groaned. His mouth closed over me and the gentleness he'd shown earlier was gone. He licked and sucked at my nipple as though he wanted to devour me.

A small cry escaped my mouth at the intensity of the sensation and my legs clasped his waist even tighter. He lifted his head long enough to bare my other breast and gave that nipple the same treatment.

Electric pleasure arced through me, straight from my nipples to my clit. My pussy clenched and I moaned.

Garrett seemed to understand that I needed more. His hand roamed over my stomach to the waistband of my joggers.

"Garrett, I want to touch you," I demanded, trying to free my wrists.

I almost managed it, but he tightened his grip, lifting his head from my breasts.

"Not now," he commanded, pressing his hand deeper into my belly. "Let me make you come."

His fingers dipped further beneath the waist of my pants until they slipped into my panties.

Garrett leveraged his body away from me, making room for his hand. A frustrated look crossed his face, as though he realized he couldn't do what he wanted and keep holding me down at the same time.

"Will you be good and stay just like this for me?" he asked.

I bit my lip but didn't answer because I wasn't sure that I could.

"I promise it will be worth it," he rumbled, dipping his fingers just low enough to brush my clit.

My entire body spasmed at the brief pleasure.

"Yes, I can stay like this," I answered, my words running over each other.

"Hands above your head," he commanded. "Hold onto the arm of the couch."

Slowly, he released my wrists, sitting back on his knees, watching me, and waiting to see what I would do.

I felt exposed, but also desperate, so I kept my arms where he left them.

His barely-there smirk appeared. "That's my good girl. You're so pretty."

I definitely wasn't a good girl, but I would act like one. For now.

Garrett's hands moved to the waistband of my pants, hooking over them, and tugging them down. It took some maneuvering, but he managed to remove them while I kept my hands exactly where he'd told me to.

He leaned over me, his eyes on the juncture of my thighs, still covered by my underwear. "You smell so good," he said.

Considering how quiet Garrett was, hearing him talk to me while he looked at my body was a huge turn on. I liked that he talked more with me than he did with others. That he was telling me how he felt about my body.

His mouth closed over my lower belly in a quick bite. I squealed in surprise, gripping the arm of the couch with my fingers, but I didn't move. There was a tug on each of my hips and I heard fabric tearing before my underwear fell away, baring me to his gaze.

His hand closed over my leg, the one closest to the back of the couch, and moved it to drape over the cushion. Then, he pushed my other leg to the side until my foot rested on the floor, spreading me wide.

He ran a finger through the wetness between my legs, spreading it up and over my clit with the rough pad of his finger. His other hand moved up to my breast, teasing my nipple. I arched my back as he toyed with me, driving me higher.

A thick finger slid into my pussy, making me gasp and shudder.

"God, you're tight," he groaned.

Garrett released my breast, bracing his hand over my head between my wrists. As his finger moved in and out of me, he leaned down and closed his lips over my breast again. The delicate bite of teeth on my nipple made me cry out because it sent a pulse of pleasure straight to my clit.

Garrett groaned against my breast and another finger pressed into me as his thumb rolled over my clit again.

Tension coiled inside me, and my legs shook with the desire to clamp down on his wrist and trap his hand exactly where it was.

He hadn't said anything about them, but I knew he wanted me to keep them open. His mouth trailed to my other breast as his fingers thrust deeper inside me, hitting a spot that made my pussy spasm.

The only sounds were the heavy sounds of our breathing and the wet slide of his fingers inside me. He worked me with his mouth and hands until I was trembling on the precipice of orgasm.

"Garrett," I gasped. "Oh, God, I'm so close."

He growled against my breast. His fingers crooked inside me, rubbing that spot deep within me as he teased my clit with his thumb. Teeth trapped the tip of my nipple in a delicate bite, and he flicked it rapidly with his tongue.

I detonated. This wasn't an orgasm, it was an explosion. Fire consumed me from the inside out as my body shook wildly beneath his. Moans tore from my throat as he continued to push my body, forcing the climax to go on and on until the edges of my vision turned black.

My heart threatened to beat out of my chest. Garrett's teeth released my nipple, and he gave it one last, long lick. His thumb slowed over my clit, bringing me down from the peak. Gasps and moans escaped my mouth as my body trembled from the vestiges of pleasure.

"Feel good?" he rumbled, rubbing his face over my breasts.

Scent marking me again, I thought.

"Yes," I panted, trying to catch my breath. "Can I touch you now?" I asked.

He opened his mouth to answer, but his phone rang in his pocket.

"Fuck," he growled. "I have to answer. It's work."

I nodded, bringing my arms down from above my head. I couldn't resist running a palm over his hip as he dug his phone out of his back pocket. He didn't make me stop, so I brought my other hand to his opposite hip as well, squeezing as I moved them down his thighs.

"Kent," he barked into the phone, his voice gruff.

I could hear the voice on the other end, but not what they were saying. It sounded like a man.

Garret stared down at me as he listened, looking more and more pained.

"Marshall, this is why I hired you. Do your job."

There was more talking.

"I'm busy," Garrett shot back.

More talking, this time loud enough for me to hear.

"No one will listen to me. They need their fucking alpha wolf, Kent. If I have to settle this, it will be with violence because I am not in the mood for this pack bullshit."

My eyes widened. Apparently, there was an issue with the wolf pack in town and his officer wasn't equipped to handle it.

"Fine. I'll be there in ten minutes."

The other man's voice was even louder when he yelled, "Are you fucking kidding me?"

Garrett snarled into the phone.

"Not you, chief. Just get here as quick as you can. I'll try not to kill anyone."

My big, bad wolf took the phone from his ear, his hot blue-green eyes glued to my still naked torso. He looked frustrated as hell.

"Fuck," he growled again.

"Not right now," I retorted, biting back a giggle at the pure frustration in his expression.

I did feel badly for him. Judging by the huge bulge in his pants, he had to be in pain.

"Do you have time for me to take care of you?" I asked, my hands clenching around his thighs as I thought about taking him into my mouth.

Garrett's head fell back, taking his eyes from me, and he groaned long and loud.

"I wish," he growled.

When he looked back down at me, the fire in his eyes was banked. His hands were gentle as he tugged my bralette back in place and pulled my tank top down. He climbed to his feet, wincing as he adjusted his erection in his pants, and bent down to pick up my pants.

My underwear was nothing but a few scraps of cotton, so I brushed them aside and slid the joggers on commando. The fleece lining brushed against my clit, still sensitive from my intense climax.

When I looked up, Garrett was sliding his fingers from his lips, growling. "Next time, I'm using my mouth."

I shivered, my nipples hardening at his words. I was half tempted to try and push him back down on the couch and tell him to do that right now.

But I remembered that he had to work.

He came closer, looming over me. "Tonight, I'm tasting you," he said.

I shivered again. How could a guy who used grunts to communicate know exactly what to say to make me wet?

"Only if I can taste you," I retorted.

Garrett groaned, his hands grabbing my hips and jerking me into his body. "Fuck," he repeated.

I wanted to laugh at the tortured tone, but I also knew exactly how he felt. I'd just come, and I was already itching to do so again.

"Tonight," I said.

"Put your shoes on." He released me and stepped back. "I'll drop you at your cottage before I handle whatever shitshow my pack has cooked up today."

As I sat on the couch to slip on my sneakers, I asked, "Does it happen often?"

"Often enough," he grumbled. "Though, now that I've found a mate, they may have to figure out how to deal with this shit themselves."

My hands froze for a second at his words.

There was one thing I hadn't told him about my conversation with Minerva. About how she thought my connection with him would unbind my magic. My fingers trembled, but I fisted them.

We could talk about that later. I wasn't even sure I wanted to mate with Garrett. It had only been three days, for God's sake.

I stood up. "Ready."

Garrett crushed me in his embrace, his lips opening over mine for a deep but brief kiss.

My head was spinning when he released my waist, grabbed my hand, and dragged me toward the door.

"If we don't leave now, we won't at all," he growled.

I didn't say it, but I was completely on board with that idea.

Chapter Fifteen

While Garrett handled whatever problem had arisen with his pack, I found myself wandering the town square, unable to sit still.

Without my permission, my feet took me back to Minerva's shop. She must have been watching out the window, because she came outside immediately.

"Goddess, Sela," she murmured, stopping a foot away from me. "I'm so sorry that I upset you like that. It wasn't my intention. Not at all. I thought you would be reassured when I explained that you weren't imagining—"

"Let's go inside," I said, interrupting her.

I was beginning to realize how sensitive the senses of supernatural creatures were, and I didn't want anyone eavesdropping on my conversation with the witch.

"Of course, of course," she said.

We went inside and the shop was as empty as it had been earlier. I wondered if she had enough customers to even stay in business here. Then again, maybe all her customers preferred to come at a certain time of day or day of the week. I had no way of knowing.

She led me back to the counter and pulled a stool out. "Please sit. Can I get you something? Tea? Water?"

I shook my head.

"Please accept my apology, Sela," she repeated. "I'm afraid I forgot the most important tenet of my magic—do no harm. I didn't see that my words were harming you and I am deeply sorry."

Minerva clasped her hands together.

"How did you know to call Garrett?" I asked, voicing the question I hadn't even realized I had.

She winced. "It's a complicated answer. It has to do with my magic."

"I promise I won't freak out this time. I'll listen."

Minerva rubbed her hands together and began pacing back and forth in front of me. "Every creature on this earth has a magical signature," she began. "Even humans. Do you follow?"

"I thought humans weren't magical?"

"Not to the extent of witches, shifters, or vampires, but all living things carry a signature. Even plants. That's why we use herbs and other plants in potions, spells, tinctures, and teas. Among other things."

I nodded. That made sense.

"When you spend time with other magical beings, especially in physical proximity, they leave a trace of their magical signature with you. I could see the police chief's signature all over you when you came by earlier. That kind of residual magic is only left when you spend hours together, usually touching in some way. I thought he would want to know what happened." She grimaced. "I'm afraid he's not very happy with me right now and I can't blame him. I didn't handle our encounter well this morning."

"I'm not angry with you," I interrupted before she could continue chastising herself.

Minerva stopped speaking and began blinking. "You're not?"

I shook my head. "No. There was no way you could have known that you were going to trigger me like that."

I took a deep breath. I'd trusted Garrett with this information when I hadn't even told my only friend in this world. Now, I was about to tell someone else.

"My parents sent me away to boarding school when I was seventeen because they were convinced that something was wrong with me. I was angry and rebellious. I wouldn't stop talking about things I saw or experienced, even though they were unwilling to listen or believe me. It was a very difficult time in my life."

Minerva's face flowed into an expression of embarrassment, then horror. "I am so very sorry I brought that up to you, Sela. If I'd had any idea..." She stopped speaking and shook her head. "That's no excuse. I should never have mentioned such a personal thing to you. I realize that you see me as a virtual stranger, but we witches tend to treat each other like family, even upon first meetings. Because, in a way, we are family. Our magic all stems from the same ancient family line. I wouldn't be surprised to see that you and I are related from many generations past. All witches are."

"How ancient is this family line?"

"Thousands of years old. Before recorded history. Magic has always existed in this world, as have witches and other magical creatures."

The concept of family was foreign to me. When I was younger and my parents thought something was wrong with me, they ceased to view me as their beloved only child and only as the family embarrassment.

Minerva came forward and laid her hand over mine. "I appreciate your forgiving soul, Sela. I promise I will watch my words when we speak in the future. I would like for us to be friends, even if you do not view me as family."

"It's difficult for me to trust people," I admitted.

Wow, I was telling her things I never told anyone. With Cari, most of these things were understood. We never truly discussed them, but she knew that I had trouble trusting people.

"I understand. I will do my best not to pressure you," she said, giving my arm a pat. "Now, will you tell me why you came by again after what happened earlier?"

I shrugged. "I'm not sure. I was restless and decided to walk around. The next thing I knew, I was here."

Minerva's golden eyes glowed. "Your heart knows you belong here, even if your head isn't ready to catch up yet."

"Will you tell me more about unlocking my power? Maybe help me figure out how it became bound in the first place?"

Her happy expression faded. "I'm more than happy to try, Sela," she said. "But I'm afraid that it might be too painful for you today. After your reaction earlier, it's clear that this is a sensitive subject for you, and I don't want to cause you more harm than I have already."

"I think that it hit me so hard because I haven't faced it. Until Garrett found me in the woods, I haven't even told another soul about what happened when I was a teenager."

"Not even Cari?" Minerva asked.

I shook my head. "No. I tried once in college. I told a boy I was dating, and he ghosted me. Everyone in my life who knew what happened treats me like I'm fragile. Or that I'll snap at any moment and do something unhinged even though I might have known them for years. My parents for example."

Minerva nodded. "I understand."

She studied me, her eyes taking on a deeper tone, as though the color of her irises fluctuated with her thoughts.

"Are you sure you want to do this now?" she asked. "We could meet tomorrow or even next week. You've already had one emotional upheaval today. I'd hate to be the catalyst for another."

"I'm sure."

"Very well. I'll make you a tea that should help us see your binding more clearly. Most witches' powers awaken with puberty, but if you didn't feel safe in your environment, it might not have manifested as a form of protection."

"Okay."

Minerva set about making another herbal concoction for me and one for herself, but this time, she put different herbs in our cups.

"I'm making your tea with ingredients meant to bring your magic to the light. To give it a bit of a boost so that it's easier to discern. My tea is one for clarity, peace, and wisdom. If I am to guide you to your awakening, I will need all three."

A few minutes later, the tea was ready, and Minerva led me back into the reading room. My heart raced when she shut the door behind us, but I took a deep breath to calm myself. What happened in here earlier did not have to happen again. I wanted to know what I was. I wanted to understand these abilities that had made my adolescence so difficult.

I also like the idea that maybe, just maybe, I belonged here in Devil

Springs. Not just because I might be Garrett's mate, but on my own merits and abilities.

"Let's take a moment to clear our minds," Minerva said. "Release all the negative thoughts that try to crowd into your mind. This is not the place for them. Now is not the time."

Her voice was low and soothing, and as dark and smooth as velvet.

"Close your eyes," she directed.

I did as she said, closing my eyes and inhaling deeply, filling up not only my lungs, but expanding my belly. When I was done, I released a stream of air in a slow, steady exhale until it was gone. Then, I did it again.

"Good," she murmured. "Now, drink your tea. At least half. And focus on the feelings you get when you see things that shouldn't be real. Or when you experience things that you can't explain."

I lifted the cup to my mouth. The tea was light and flavorful as it slid over my tongue and down my throat. There was a slight bitter after-taste, but it vanished quickly.

I focused on the tingle I always felt at the base of my neck when someone lied to me. To how that tingle spread when I saw another magical being. I might not have understood what I was seeing in my mind, but my magic recognized it. That was why it reacted.

After a few moments, Minerva whispered, "You may open your eyes."

I did as she asked and nearly gasped. My skin glowed with golden light. And when I looked at Minerva, she was surrounded by light as well, but hers was a silvery white. Where I appeared as the sun, she was the moon, tranquil and bright.

"You're glowing," I whispered back, not wanting to break the fragile moment.

"So are you."

"Why?" I asked.

"Your magic has called to mine." Her eyes studied me, more calculating than they had been earlier. "I can see your bindings clearly. They're centered around your heart."

I looked down and gasped when I saw thin black and grey lines wrapped around the center of my chest.

"How do I remove them?" I asked.

"Your pain is what bound your magic," Minerva continued. "You shut down anything that could hurt you more, closed off your heart. It also took your magic with it. Emotions fuel our powers as witches. Because emotion influences intention and intention is the key when using magic."

"How do I free my power?" I asked.

Minerva blinked and the glow surrounding both of us faded. "You must open your heart again. You must allow yourself to feel emotions, both negative and positive. Neither can exist without the other. But because of the negative emotions you experienced at such a young age, you chose to protect your heart by shutting them all away."

She wasn't lying. I could sense it.

"That's all, huh?" I asked, my tone dry.

Minerva smiled. It was kind and empathetic. "It's a frightening thought, I know. Opening yourself up to pain after you finally escaped it. But it is the only way."

"I'm not even sure I know how," I said.

"You do," Minerva replied quickly. "You have opened yourself up to Cari. That's why some of your magic is already leaking. When you open yourself the rest of the way, your power will be completely free."

"That doesn't tell me how."

She smiled. "I think you'll know when the time is right. But you have to listen to that inner voice. The one that insisted everything you saw as a child was real. That magic was real. That inner voice will tell you when the time is right."

I made a face at her. "Gee. Thanks, Yoda."

Minerva laughed and it was like smoke in the room. She could make a fortune narrating audiobooks.

Huh. Did all supernatural beings have incredible voices? Maybe I'd suggest the audiobook thing to her when I got to know her better.

"Thank you, Minerva," I said, getting to my feet. "I hope you're right."

Her smile turned mysterious. "I'm always right."

It was my turn to laugh. "It would be nice to have that kind of confidence."

A strange look crossed her face. "No, not always."

Minerva also got to her feet, gathering up our teacups. "Please come see me again soon," she said, following me out of the reading room.

"I think I will," I answered.

She took a moment to carry the cup over to a small sink behind the counter of the front section of her shop.

I thought of another question as she walked me toward the door of the shop.

"Minerva, is it common for shifters to take humans as their mates?" I asked.

She stopped, blinking at me. "What?"

"Shifters take mates, right? Are they often human?" I asked.

She shook her head. "Not often, no. It has been known to happen though." She paused and cleared her throat. "Are you saying that Garrett has taken you as his mate?"

"He says that I'm his mate, but he also says he won't claim me until I'm sure I'll want to stay."

"Oh, dear," Minerva whispered.

A small pain spiked through my chest. "Oh, dear?" I asked.

She looked torn, as though she didn't want to say anything else. "Minerva?"

The witch sighed. "I'm sorry, Sela. I'm not trying to upset you twice in one day, but, when I say shifters rarely take humans as mates, it's because it very rarely ends well. Being human means that they don't feel the same attachment their mate feels. They don't have that instinct, that drive, to constantly be close to their mate. Nor do they have the unconditional love and irresistible attraction for their mate that a shifter has. Combine that with the possessiveness and potential violence of their animal..." She swallowed hard. "It typically ends in blood and with the shifter having to be put down."

Fear moved through my body. No wonder Garrett was hesitant to claim me. He knew that he would never want to let me go and that he would be irrationally possessive. If he behaved that way right now, I'd probably run for the hills, which sounded like a dangerous reaction.

"What about shifter couples that mate? Are they happy? I mean, fate chooses their mate for them. Is fate ever wrong?"

Minerva's eyes were wide as she answered me. "Fate is never wrong, but each shifter has a human side. Their animals may be compatible, but their personalities may not. Once the mating instincts fade, some couples do find that they don't mesh well while in human form."

My secret internal hope wilted further.

Garrett said he would answer all my questions about mating, but he hadn't mentioned any of this. Granted, I hadn't thought to ask him about it yet, but I damn sure would tonight.

"Thank you for your honesty," I said to her.

She looked worried as she studied me. "May I hug you, Sela?"

Instead of saying anything, I stepped forward and wrapped my arms around her shoulders. She was so much shorter than me that her head rested over my heart.

"I'm glad you came into my shop today," she murmured when she released me. "I hope I see you again very soon."

"I'm glad I met you, too. I'm sure I'll be back in a day or two with more questions."

"I admire a curious mind," she replied. "I'll be here."

I left her shop, simultaneously feeling better and worse.

I now knew that there was nothing wrong with me. And that I needed to trust my instincts.

But I was also worried about any possible future I could have with Garrett. Which made me want to roll my eyes.

Three days. I'd known the man three days! Who could determine if someone was the love of their life in three days?

And why was I talking about love, even inside my own head? I couldn't love him after three days.

Could I?

I was so lost inside my own head that I didn't see Leo before I crashed headlong into him.

"Sela!" he said, his hands resting on my arms. "Are you okay?"

"Yeah, sorry," I said, shaking my head to try and focus. "Did I hurt you?"

"I'm fine. I've been looking for you."

I tilted my head back and looked up at him. He wasn't as tall as Garrett, but he did have a couple of inches on me.

"What? Why?"

His expression closed off. "I can't talk about it out in the open."

Suspicion shot down my spine and I took a step back. "I'm not sure I want to go anywhere private with you for a discussion."

His face fell. "I understand. We can go to the police station and Garrett can be in on the talk if you want. In fact, it would probably be for the best. You've been spending a lot of time together, so he should know to be on his guard."

"On his guard?" I asked.

Before Leo could answer, a big, black SUV screeched to a halt by the sidewalk where we stood. The back door flew open, and two men piled out. Two huge men.

Leo snarled, crouching in front of me. "Back off," he said, his voice suddenly two octaves deeper and much louder.

The two men kept coming and Leo roared, leaping toward them.

As he did, a hard arm banded around my neck and a cloth was slapped over my mouth.

"Sleep," a male voice whispered in my ear.

The last thing I heard was Leo roar again. This time in pain.

Chapter Sixteen

onsciousness returned slowly. Mostly because of the pain that thrummed in my temples.

This was worse than any hangover I'd ever felt. I groaned and lifted a hand to my head.

Well, I tried to lift a hand to my head, but it wouldn't move.

Frowning, I cracked open my eyes, hissing out a breath when the bright sunlight assaulted me. Why couldn't I move my arm?

I turned my face away from the light and tried opening my eyes again. This time, they cooperated. Confused, I took in the roughly cut walls of rock around me. Where was I?

"You're in a very special place."

I squinted toward the back of the cave, where the daylight didn't reach. I was currently near the mouth, sitting directly in the late afternoon sun.

A woman emerged from the shadows. Tall, blond, statuesque. She looked like a movie star from the 1940's, but she dressed like a businesswoman. Her only nod to the uneven terrain was a pair of black boots with a low, square heel. Every other inch of her was chic and cold. Down to her glacial blue eyes.

She also looked vaguely familiar, but I couldn't place where I knew her from.

"What?" I asked.

"You asked where you were. I told you."

She came closer to me, crouching a couple of feet away. Her blonde hair was pulled back in smooth twist and her make-up was perfect and understated.

"Why did you bring me here?" I asked. "And who the hell are you?"

Now that I was fully conscious, my memory was returning.

"Did you hurt Leo?" I asked, jerking against the rope that bound my wrists to a stainless steel eye screwed into the floor.

"My wayward son is fine. Maybe a bit battered and bruised, but he'll heal quickly enough." Her eyes were like shards of ice as she talked about her child.

I realized then that this was Leona, the woman who'd intended to kidnap Cari and use her to force Daniel to resign as mayor. And she'd sent men to take me and allowed them to harm her son.

Sure, he was huge and a shifter, but he was still her boy. She'd carried him in her body, but she spoke about him as though he were no more than a means to an end.

Chills rushed over my body. This woman had ice running through her veins instead of blood.

"What you should be concerned about is yourself," she continued.

She could have been talking about the weather for all the emotion she showed.

"But I will answer your first question," she said. "I brought you here to help me accomplish a goal."

A man emerged from behind her, brushing his hands together as though they were dirty.

"The altar is ready, Leona."

The woman in question rose to her full height, which was a good three inches taller than me. Her frigid blue eyes remained on me.

"Now, little witch," she said. "Are you going to come with me peacefully or are you going to force me to do something that neither of us will enjoy?"

I was tempted to make as much trouble as possible. It was in my nature. But the look in her eyes told me that she would hurt me, possibly permanently maim me, and wouldn't lose a moment of sleep.

"I'll come peacefully if you'll answer one more question."

She gave me an arrogant nod, as though she were a queen deigning to indulge a peasant.

"Are you planning to hurt me?"

Her brows rose and she glanced at the man. "Will he hurt her, Sommerton?"

The man came closer, looking down at me. He wasn't as aloof as Leona. No, he looked...excited, which did nothing to lessen my anxiety.

"There may be some pain, but we do not plan to kill you," he said.

I waited to see if the tingle on my nape appeared, but it remained blessedly cool. He was telling the truth.

"Does that answer your question?" Leona asked, a self-satisfied smirk spreading across her lips.

"Yes," I answered.

I glanced down at my bound hands. There wasn't enough rope for me to stand.

"You'll have to untie me," I said.

The man, Sommerton, came forward and waved a hand over the rope, whispering words I couldn't understand.

Suddenly, a length of the rope appeared in his hand, and it was now attached to my bindings...which were no longer threaded through the hook.

I stared at both of them, completely at a loss for words.

"Up," Leona commanded.

God, the woman was insufferable, but I had promised to come peacefully if she wasn't going to injure me.

I shoved myself up, brushing the dirt off my legs and butt as I did.

"Lead the way, *garçon*," I said to the man.

He glared at me, jerking the rope so hard that it nearly pulled me off balance. I tripped over my feet for a couple of steps but was able to trail behind him as he led me into the shadows at the back of the cave.

The hall in front of us was wide and obviously man-made. The rock was cut too cleanly for this to be naturally occurring.

We walked for a while, the only sounds our footsteps and our breathing. It had to be thirty or forty minutes before we emerged from the hall into a huge chamber with a soaring ceiling and torches lit at regular intervals along the walls. I was relieved because the only light in the passage had been a ball of energy that Sommerton conjured to hover above us. Leona didn't seem to need it. Stupid shifter supersight.

A squat, square rock sat in the middle of the chamber, each corner set with a huge oil urn that was lit. All four of them flickered with flames that seemed unnaturally bright. That must be the altar.

As we got closer, I realized the altar was much larger than I originally thought. It wasn't very tall, just coming up to my waist, but the surface was probably ten feet by six feet.

"Lie down," Leona said, her voice echoing throughout the chamber. I hesitated.

Sommerton jerked the rope again. This time, I allowed it to pull me forward, so I "accidentally" stomped all over his feet and kicked his shins.

"Bitch," he hissed, shoving me back.

"Stop jerking me around and I won't run into you. It's not like I can use my arms for balance, asshole," I shot back.

Before he could reply, Leona's voice cut between us. "Enough." She gestured to the altar. "Lie down."

I brushed past the man, making sure to knock into him with my shoulder. He grunted and I saw his free hand tighten into a fist.

I rolled my eyes as I stretched out on one side of the flat rock.

"In the center," Leona commanded.

I scooted over on my hands and butt until I rested in the center of the stone. The man tugged my arms up until they were stretched over my head. Almost uncomfortably so. He murmured another phrase in a language I couldn't understand, and the rope was suddenly attached to another steel eyebolt at the top of the altar.

Something wrapped around my ankles, and I looked down to see two new ropes, one for each leg, also tied to eyebolts jutting from the altar. My legs were stretched out, but not spread wide, so I wasn't completely uncomfortable.

Leona nodded to Sommerton. "Begin."

The man stood at my head, lifting his arms in an exaggerated pose, and began speaking in that foreign language. It wasn't anything I'd ever heard before. I could feel the air stirring around me. My skin prickled as it intensified. Then the pinpricks turned to burns. I sucked in a sharp breath, trying not to fight against the sensation. Somehow, I knew that would make it hurt worse.

There was a heaviness to the air, and it began to coalesce right above me. A small knot of black smoke appeared, a greyish purple light emitting from the center. The knot grew into a ball, then larger until it was the size of a car tire.

The burning sensation on my skin grew more intense. I gasped, my back arching, as a strange feeling zipped through me. It felt as if it was yanking at something inside me, but it couldn't quite pull it free.

There was another pull, this time harder, but nothing happened. I glanced up at Sommerton and saw that his face was red with exertion. He began yelling the words and the heaviness in the air intensified.

I assumed he'd poured more magic into whatever spell he was trying to cast. The uncomfortable scrape hit within me again, this time deeper. I cried out, my back arching hard on the stone as my guts felt as though they were being ripped from my body.

Still, there was no relief. Whatever he was doing wasn't working.

Sommerton's voice grew softer and slower. The ball of black smoke and purple light above me dissipated, trailing off into nothing.

Sommerton bent over, his hands resting on the edge of the altar above my head. He was panting.

"It didn't work," he said. "Her power is bound."

"So, break the bonds," Leona said.

Sommerton grimaced. "It's not that simple. Whoever bound her power is strong. I've never seen a spell like it. It's as if it's anchored to her heart. It will be tricky to remove it without killing her."

"If she dies, she dies," Leona said, shrugging as though my life meant nothing to her.

"You promised you wouldn't kill me," I yelled, tugging at the rope.

Sommerton waved a hand over my face and a piece of cloth wrapped over my mouth, gagging me.

"I can't do that," he said.

Leona turned and fixed him with a harsh stare.

"If I kill her and it doesn't work, then how will we open the seal?" he asked.

Seal? What seal?

I couldn't ask though because I had that stupid gag over my mouth.

Leona's harsh stare came to me, then back to Sommerton. "Then, you'd better think of something to destroy the binding. Something that won't kill her."

The "or else" was unspoken, but still clear enough.

"Give me an hour or two. I should be able to create a potion to release her power."

"For your sake, I hope it works," Leona said.

Even I could hear Sommerton swallow hard, but I just scowled up at him. The asshole deserved to be scared. He knew what he was doing was wrong. He just didn't care.

Leona walked back out of the room, heading toward the mouth of the cave.

Sommerton lowered his head and sighed. His eyes met mine, but I just squinted at him with the most hateful glare I could manage.

He scoffed and pushed himself up. Then, he walked away. I tried to shift my head to watch him, but he was moving directly above my head, and I couldn't get enough slack in the rope to swivel around to watch him. I did manage to rub my cheek against my arm and roll the gag away from my mouth and down to my neck.

A moment later, he returned with a bowl in one hand and a small knife in the other.

I tried to shy away when he set the bowl next to my left wrist, but he opened his spread hand right above me. My body was suddenly frozen to the rock. I couldn't even blink.

I watched as he lifted my left wrist, shoved up my sleeve, and sliced down my forearm. It wasn't right over my vein, but blood welled quickly enough. The pain was sharp and cold, but I couldn't cry out. I couldn't even take a deep breath. Every part of me was stilled. Except for my heart.

That still beat, likely to keep the blood flowing.

When the bowl was half full, Sommerton murmured a couple more words. The knife in his hand turned orange, as though he'd placed it in a forge. As he lowered it, I realized what he was about to do and tried to scream, to jerk free.

But my body refused to obey.

I could only lie there and feel the agony of the red-hot blade as he cauterized the wound.

"You shouldn't have been such a bitch," he whispered near my ear. "Or I would have made sure this didn't hurt at all."

As he stepped away, he released me. I sucked in ragged breaths now that my lungs were working again.

I wished that my power had awakened when he was hurting me, because the way I was feeling at the moment, I would have squashed him like a bug.

Considering he said only someone extremely powerful could have bound my magic, I probably could have done it. Because, according to Minerva, I was the one who did it to myself. I'd bound my own power.

And I was obviously stronger than him if he couldn't break it himself.

As I laid on that altar, listening to him moving around the chamber just out of sight, I reached within me for that place I'd felt earlier. And I tugged.

I could feel the binding then. In my mind's eye, it looked like hundreds upon hundreds of black and grey threads wrapped around a pulsing golden heart. I realized that heart was my magic.

Now, I just had to set it free.

One thread at a time.

* * *

My mind was hazy. Sweat dripped off my temples and into my hair despite the chilly temperature of the cavern.

Removing the threads around my magic was proving to be trickier than I anticipated. The first few were easy enough, but each one thereafter felt like peeling a sliver of skin from my body.

It hurt. God, did it hurt. Why hadn't Minerva warned me how difficult this would be? Or how painful?

My body trembled with the effort it took to remove another thread. When I was done, every muscle went lax. I had to rest. At this rate, I would free my power but have no energy left to fight my way out of here. If I could even figure out how to use my magic in a fight by then.

Sommerton was still puttering around where I couldn't see him. Every so often, I would hear him mutter something to himself as he worked. It had been at least an hour since he'd cut my arm and dripped my blood into a bowl.

Rocks skittered as rapid footsteps came down the passageway to the cavern. With some of the threads undone from my binding, I could sense the essence of the person coming. It was Leona.

The hope that had flared in my chest immediately extinguished.

"Have you solved the problem?" she asked.

She was speaking to Sommerton, but she was hovering over me, staring at my sweaty face and body.

"What did you do to her?" she asked. She sounded bland and curious rather than angry.

"I took a bit of her blood," Sommerton replied, still banging around where I couldn't see him.

"Why did you burn her?"

"To cauterize the wound so she wouldn't bleed all over the place."

I decided now was a good time to try and distract both of them.

"What seal are you planning to break?" I asked. "And why in the hell did you decide you needed me to break it?"

They ignored me.

So, I decided to be as annoying as possible.

"Mary had a little lamb, little lamb, little laaaaaaamb!" I sang-screeched.

They stopped talking and stared down at me like I'd lost my mind.

"Yeah, I'm still here and I asked a damn question."

Sommerton moved his hand, as though he were going to bespell me again, but Leona stopped him.

"What were your questions?" she asked, her tone placating.

"What seal are you breaking? And why am I the one who must help you break it?"

"We're freeing the blood god," she answered. "The seal is what kept him trapped for millennia. And you are the key because you contain bound magic. Your awakening will supply enough power to break the seal."

"So you're going to steal my magic?" I asked.

Sommerton rolled his eyes, scoffing. "No. Just the initial burst. Don't you know anything?"

I narrowed my eyes on him, feeling that space inside me shiver, shaking loose another black thread around my power. "I thought I was human my entire life until today. I'm ignorant because I had no one to teach me. What's your excuse for being an irredeemable asshole?"

He reared back, clenching a fist. I waited until it was almost on my face before I rolled to the side and let his hand smash into the rock beneath me.

"Ahhhhh!" he screeched. "You bitch!"

He pulled back his other fist, but Leona was between us, and she grabbed his uninjured hand.

"Stop, you idiot. You're giving her exactly what she wants." She shoved him back and he stumbled, falling on his ass. "Save your tantrum for later. Right now, she's the key."

Sommerton glared at me, his eyes glittering with malice.

I ignored him, focusing on Leona. "Who is the blood god and why do you want to wake him up?"

She sighed. "I'm indulging your curiosity because I believe you might be more willing to help me achieve my goal. But if you continue to provoke Sommerton, I won't be able to protect you for much longer."

"I'm genuinely curious. Please tell me why this is so important."

Leona came and sat on the edge of the stone altar, her hip next to mine. I could see her face easily.

"The blood god is exactly what he sounds like—he controls blood magic. The same magic that creates witches, destines mates for one another, and does a whole host of things in our world. It is the oldest and most powerful magic. And the blood god has ultimate control over that power. He is beyond warlocks, witches, and enchantresses. He could destroy them all with a mere thought."

My eyes widened. "If he's that dangerous, why are you waking him up?"

"Because we need him." Her tone said she thought I was an idiot.

"For what?" I asked.

"For one, to bring us supernaturals back into the forefront of society again. We once controlled cities, states, even entire countries. Now, we are forced to hide what we are for fear of frightening the humans and having them turn on us. They outnumber us and therefore could destroy us with sheer quantity."

Oh, yes, that sounded great. Powerful supernatural beings should absolutely be in control of the government because they were so obviously in touch with reality. Not.

"Is there another reason?" I asked.

"To get rid of this fated mates nonsense. No one could be happy stuck with someone they knew for all of three minutes before they were mated. My mate is weak and pathetic. And now, my son is just like him. They think we should work with those inferior to us. Not just witches and other weak powers, but with humans as well. That we should learn to coexist rather than rule." she sighed, throwing her head back. "Those with power should be in charge, not hiding in the shadows, afraid of what might happen if they're discovered."

"You're not happy with your mate?" I asked. "From what I understood, that's extremely rare."

Leona rolled her eyes. "Only because these weak-minded idiots don't question the magic. They claim it's destiny. Fate. But, in reality, it's just similar magic recognizing similar magic. Nothing more complicated than that. It doesn't guarantee a lifetime of happiness as they think it does."

My stomach shriveled. She just voiced my worst fear of Garrett's insistence that we were mates. That, one day down the road, we would no longer be happy together, but still bound. Stuck together for eternity.

Before I could ask her anything further, an eerie howl echoed down the passage to the chamber.

Leona leapt to her feet, sharp claws extending from her hands and her face began to shift. A split second later, I was looking at a human woman's body with a lioness's head attached. It was freaky as hell.

"How did they find us?" she growled.

152

"With my help."

My eyes wheeled around, and I saw Minerva standing on the other side of the altar, her hands lifted beside her, palm up.

"Not so fast," she snapped, shoving her right hand toward Sommerton. She gestured toward him, and I twisted my head around to see what was happening when he screamed.

He flew across the chamber and, just before he would have hit the wall, he vanished in a flash of light and puff of smoke.

"That coward," Minerva spat.

She turned toward Leona, lifting both of her hands toward the lioness. But Leona tossed something at the altar. There was a delicate tinkle of glass and then flames roared to life all around the squat stone.

I shrieked and tried to jerk my arms and legs toward the center, but the rope held fast. It wasn't even scorching beneath the flames.

I tried to fight the pull of the ropes, but it was no use. The inferno was rising, and it was going to burn me alive.

Minerva cursed and a layer of ice formed around the altar. It took a few minutes, but the flames were eventually subdued.

As the smoke and steam dissipated, I coughed and blinked. Leona had vanished and Minerva was the only other person in the chamber with me.

"I am so glad to see you," I said to her, coughing and choking.

She waved a hand over my hands and feet. The ropes holding me vanished. I tried to sit up, but my arms and legs were tingling violently as the blood rushed back into my extremities.

Minerva came over to the altar and helped me sit up. Her hands rubbed up and down my arms, helping the blood flow to increase. After a few painful moments, the tingling faded. My limbs were still weak though. Whether from the work I'd done to free my magic or from the adrenaline crash, I couldn't tell.

"How did you find me?" I asked her.

"I found Leo in the alley behind my store after they took you. I managed to help him regain consciousness. When he told me what happened, I went over to Cari's cottage and found your hairbrush. I used some of your hair to cast a spell and find you. Then, I gathered the cavalry, and we all made our way here." She gave me a rueful smile. "We would have been here sooner, but Edgar set a few booby traps in the woods surrounding this cave."

"Who's Edgar?"

Minerva grinned. "Sommerton. He's always hated his name, which means I go out of my way to call him by it every chance I get."

I laughed, wrapping my arms around my waist. "I always liked the name Edgar, but only because I like Edgar Allen Poe's works."

Minerva laughed, too. "That's exactly who he was named after."

"What an insult to one of my favorite authors," I muttered.

Another howl bounced down the stone passageway and filled the chamber.

"There's your mate," Minerva said, a small smile on her lips.

My chest ached at her words. Right over my heart.

I wanted Garrett to be my mate. But I was also afraid. After talking to Minerva today and then to Leona, I was terrified of being trapped.

Sure, Garrett seemed great right now. Most men did in the beginning. But as time passed, things changed. True natures were revealed because they were no longer on their best behavior. I knew there were men in this world who didn't behave like that, but I'd yet to date one of them.

It had taken me a very long time to learn to love myself and to only accept what I deserved in a relationship. I wasn't going to throw all that away because of a romantic notion of fated mates.

Was I?

There was a scrabble of claws on the rock floor leading into the chamber. A few seconds later, two enormous wolves and a mountain lion burst through the entrance. I immediately recognized Garrett's wolf. He was as blonde as Garrett was in human form.

The other wolf was similar in size and coloring. Somehow, I knew it was a she-wolf. I wondered if it was Garrett's sister, Poppy.

The mountain lion stopped at the edge of the room, staying back from me.

Garrett skidded to a halt at the altar, nudging Minerva away, and hopping up onto the stone. He snuffled around me, sniffing every inch of my legs, torso, and arms. Until he reached my left wrist. He took my fingers between his teeth, incredibly gentle, and turned my palm over so that my inner forearm was visible. The burn was still angry and red.

Garrett's wolf snarled viciously.

"Oh, dear," Minerva said. "Why didn't you tell me you were hurt, Sela?"

"I was a little distracted by the flames trying to set my hair on fire," I retorted.

Garrett growled again, snapping his teeth. Not at me or Minerva, but in the air. He was clearly pissed as hell.

"Let me see what I can do," she said, reaching for me.

Garrett turned on her, snarling again.

I tugged his tail, which made him whirl toward me, his blue-green eyes wheeling in his skull.

"Calm down, Wolfie," I said. "She's going to try and heal me, not hurt me."

Garrett whined and laid down on the stone next to my hip, resting his head on my lap. I sighed and brushed the fingers of my right hand through his fur.

"It's okay, baby," I said. "I'm safe now."

The wolf cuddled closer but didn't move when Minerva reached for my wrist again. But he watched her intently, never taking his gaze off her hands as she turned my arm this way and that.

"That is a nasty burn. It's deep, too," she said, her voice pained. "I can heal it, but it will take a couple of sessions." Her lips curved as her bright gold eyes returned to mine. "You probably won't even have a scar when I'm done."

"Thank you, Minerva," I said.

"It's nothing."

She placed her palm over the burn, keeping a few inches of space between her flesh and mine. A silver light emanated from her palm, a cool breeze wafted over my throbbing wound. When she stopped a few moments later, her skin was pale and there was a bead of sweat at her temple.

"There, that's already much better," she said.

I glanced down and my eyes widened. The burn was no longer angry and red, but looked as if had occurred a few days ago rather than less than two hours.

Minerva swayed.

"Are you okay?" I asked.

She nodded. "Healing takes it out of you, but this place makes it worse." She shuddered. "It's made to devour magic. Especially blood magic."

"Do you know what this place is?" I asked.

Minerva shook her head. "No, but I can feel the spells working on me."

Maybe that was why I couldn't free my magic. And why Sommerton couldn't break through my power's bindings.

"Then we should get out of here."

Garrett rose and jumped off the altar. He used his teeth to tug my leg over the side of the stone. Then, he bumped his back against my thigh.

"I think he wants you to ride him," Minerva said.

Garrett's wolf yipped.

"How?" I asked, looking between him and Minerva.

She helped me lay on his back, astride him as though he were a horse, but with my hands clutching the fur on the scruff of his neck.

"Go slowly, Garrett," she said. "Your mate is feeling weak at the moment."

The wolf chuffed as though he understood.

Minerva swayed again and the giant mountain lion approached her, butting her leg with its head.

"Thank you, Marshall," she said primly.

Then, Minerva placed herself on his back in a similar position as mine.

The three shifters shared a look before they took off down the passageway.

Chapter Seventeen

It took longer than I expected to make our way down the side of the mountain and through the woods to where Garrett's SUV was parked.

Another Devil Springs PD vehicle was parked behind it. It was an older year model, but still well kept.

Garrett stopped by his vehicle, as did the other wolf.

The mountain lion stopped to let Minerva climb off its back before it disappeared around the other vehicle.

I watched as Garrett shifted back into human form. He opened the door of the SUV and pulled out a pair of gym shorts, which he jerked on quickly. Then, he shook out a long t-shirt and held it out to the other wolf. The other animal took it and headed back out into the trees. A few moments later, a young woman reappeared, wearing the t-shirt, which ended up being a dress on her, and barefoot.

Minerva walked over to us as the woman approached.

She was shorter than Garrett, but not quite as tall as me.

"I'm Poppy," she said, look up at me. "Garrett's sister. I wish we'd met under better circumstances, but I'm still happy to meet you, Sela," she said.

I held out my hand. "I've heard a lot about you from Cari and Garrett."

C.C. WOOD

She smiled at me, her hand gripping mine firmly. "And they've both told me a lot about you, too."

Her eyes were more green than Garrett's and they twinkled with mischief.

"Thank you for coming to help me," I said.

"Hey, you're family now," she said. "We'll always have your back."

The hope that had withered within my chest began to bloom again. Family. Not just family, but people that cared enough to show up when I needed them. It was something I'd longed for most of my adult life. Cari fulfilled most of that yearning, but I'd always wanted more than one sibling. It would be nice to have another woman in my life that I considered my sister.

Garrett appeared beside me.

"Thanks."

Poppy leaned over and kissed his cheek. "Anytime, big bro." She turned toward the second cruiser. "Marshall! Give me a ride back to town!"

A lean man appeared around the vehicle, dressed in a police uniform. He scowled at her. "I'm not your car service, woman."

Poppy ignored him and continued walking toward his car, still barefoot. The officer scowled and dug around in the back of his vehicle, coming out with a pair of slides.

"Put these on your feet," he commanded.

Poppy sighed but did as he asked.

Minerva waved at me as she climbed into the front seat of the other officer's cruiser. Poppy slid into the back, also waving.

"Come see me soon. I need to finish healing your arm," Minerva called out the open window as they drove away, leaving me alone with Garrett.

It suddenly occurred to me how close I'd come to being hurt. My body started trembling and tears filled my eyes.

I took a ragged breath and two huge arms closed around me, pulling me into Garrett's chest.

"I've got you," he said.

I leaned against him. Now that I knew where my magic was and could feel how it was bound within me, I could feel how it pulsed when

I was close to him. My power liked him. It strained behind the black threads, trying to reach him.

"Thank you for coming for me," I said.

"Always."

I cried for a few minutes, letting out some of the stress and fear. Garrett's hand patted my hair.

When I finally sniffled to a stop, he asked, "Are you ready to go home?"

"Yes." I tilted my head back to look up at him. "Are you going to give me cookies and hot cocoa again?"

"If you want, but I was leaning more toward spaghetti and a stiff drink."

"Can I have both?" I asked.

"You can have whatever you want."

* * *

Garrett didn't take me to the cottage in town. He took me to his house.

As soon as we walked inside, he guided me to the bathroom in his bedroom. The one I hadn't seen before.

There was a huge, deep tub in one corner. It was large enough to accommodate a man Garrett's size, which meant I'd basically be swimming in it.

Garrett went over and immediately started filling it up with hot water, dumping a heap of Epsom salts from the bag on the edge of the tub.

I watched him, my body aching and my emotions numb.

He came over to me, his expression serious. "I know you're tired, but I really need you to take a bath," he said.

I wasn't opposed to the idea of soaking in that enormous tub. Not at all. But I didn't understand why it seemed so important to him.

"Why?" I asked.

"Because I can smell them on you and it's driving my wolf insane. He wants to hunt them both down and rip—" Garrett stopped speaking and inhaled sharply. "I think it will calm me down. And maybe help you feel a little better, too."

"Okay," I answered.

Garrett lifted my shirt over my head. I let my arms come up, not even trying to stop him. I was too tired to worry about what he thought about my body at the moment.

His hands were tender as he crouched down to help me remove my shoes and socks. My leggings and underwear were next, leaving me naked in the middle of his bathroom.

I wrapped my arms around my waist and shivered. The air was cool in here.

"I need something so I can put up my hair," I muttered, not wanting to deal with it getting wet.

"Your purse is in my car. Do you have anything in there that will help?"

I hadn't even thought about that after I'd been taken. It must have fallen off during the struggle. I was glad he brought it.

"Yes."

"I'll be right back," Garrett said.

I wandered over to the tub sat on the edge, leaning my back against the cold tile of the wall. As soon as my skin made contact, I hissed and sat up again. I glanced over my shoulder and saw several long, raw welts running down my back. I must have wiggled too much on the altar when I was trying to free my magic and avoid getting hit by an enraged warlock.

The hot water was going to sting like a bitch when I got in the tub, but the Epsom salts would help me heal.

Garrett reappeared, my bag in his hand. Sure enough, the strap was broken. He knelt in front of me, holding the bag out. I unzipped the front pocket, dug around until I found one of the extra elastics I kept there, and pulled it out.

He carried my bag over to the bathroom counter. "I'll get you a shirt to wear when you're done," he said.

"Could you grab some antibiotic ointment for my back, too?" I asked.

Garrett appeared in front of me so quickly that I jerked and gasped. He caught my elbows, bringing me to my feet, and gently turned me so that he could look at my back.

160

He growled low in his throat as he studied the injuries there. "Did they do this to you?"

I shook my head. "I must have rubbed it raw when I was trying to escape."

A low snarl filled the bathroom.

"They're dead," he said, his tone lethal. "No one touches my mate. No one hurts my mate."

"Doesn't killing people go against your policies at the police department?" I asked.

"Not here in Devil Springs."

Yikes. Okay, I needed to diffuse this situation quickly.

"I think I'd prefer for them to rot in jail for a very long time. It'll make them suffer longer."

Garrett stared down at my face, but I had the distinct sensation that it was his wolf looking through his eyes. There was a wildness there that was absent most of the time.

"I want their blood," he insisted, his voice a low snarl.

I stepped back, pulling my hair up into a messy bun. "I stand by what I said. I'd rather them rot in a dungeon somewhere for a very long time. That way they really suffer."

Garrett didn't say anything else. He cradled my arms in a delicate grip as I stepped into the tub. The water was nearly scalding, which meant it was perfect.

I lowered myself into the water, hissing as the water touched the raw spots on my back. But it still felt good.

"You good?" he asked.

I sighed. "Yes."

"I'll make some food."

"I could eat." I smiled at him and leaned back against the side of the bathtub.

He watched me for a long moment before he left the room.

I waited until he was gone because the smile left my face. While I was captive, I hadn't wanted to admit how scared I was.

But I hadn't doubted for a moment that Garrett would come looking for me. Which was strange. I'd never had that kind of faith in a man before. Not even my own father.

I soaked in the tub for a while before Garrett came in with my phone in one hand and a short, squat glass in the other.

"Vodka rocks," he said, setting the glass on the wide lip of the tub. "And Cari wanted to talk to you."

I winced, feeling like a heel. I should have called her as soon as Garrett brought me here.

I took the phone and immediately said, "I'm so sorry, Cari. I should have called. I was just...discombobulated."

A muted sob drifted out of the speaker, which made my eyes tear up immediately.

"Are you okay?" she asked, her voice thick with tears.

"Other than a couple of bruises and welts, I'm not hurt at all."

"I'm so sorry I wasn't with Garrett. He and Daniel refused to let me come along."

"Cari, it was dangerous. I wouldn't have wanted you there. You would have been in as much danger as I was."

"But you would rappel from a helicopter with commandos for me!" she cried. "I want to do the same for you."

I looked at Garrett with confusion. He just shrugged, which was absolutely no help.

"Cari, I love you more than any sister I could have had. But I wouldn't rappel from a helicopter for you. I'm afraid of heights. I would, however, walk through fire for you." I paused. "Or around a fire, maybe."

She sniffled and laughed at the same time. "I know what you're trying to do, and it won't work."

"What won't work?" I asked, pretending innocence.

"You're trying to make me feel better, but I don't. And it's my job to make you feel better! I'm your best friend." She cleared her throat. "So, tell me where you are and I'll come pick you up."

I opened my mouth to tell her that wasn't necessary, that I was okay, and Garrett was taking care of me, but my so-called mate reached out and grabbed the phone from my hand, lifting it to his ear.

"I've got her, Cari."

I couldn't understand what she was saying because I didn't have heightened shifter hearing, but she was yelling.

"Cari, I've got her," he repeated.

There was more yelling, and Garrett frowned fiercely. "Zeke and Poppy are trying to follow Leona's trail. Minerva is on the hunt for Sommerton. And I'm exactly where I need to be, which is with my mate." A pause. "Zeke Marshall is one of my officers. You haven't met him yet."

There was silence after that. Cari must have lowered her voice because I couldn't hear her words at all now.

"I will, Cari. I promise."

Garrett lowered the phone, tapping the screen with his thumb.

I scowled at him. "I was talking to my friend," I said.

"I know, but you don't need to be calming her down. You need to be resting and recovering from being fucking kidnapped," he rumbled. He sounded pissed again.

"You also told my best friend that I was your mate," I continued, completely ignoring what he said.

"I did. What I want to know, is why didn't you?"

I frowned even more fiercely. "Because I wanted to decide on my own if I even believed in fated mates. As soon as I told her, she would have spent all her time trying to convince me that having a mate was the best thing ever and how awesome it would be because then we'd both be able to live here."

He crossed his arms over his chest and his face said he didn't believe a word I said.

I stood up in the tub, but my foot slid out from beneath me and I scrambled to catch my balance. Before I could fall on the floor, two strong arms caught me, pinning me to Garrett's chest.

"Careful," he barked.

The water from my skin soaked through his white t-shirt, plastering it to his body and turning it transparent.

I looked up at him, our faces only a few inches apart. He took a deep breath, moving his head to press his nose to the side of my neck.

"I almost lost you," he murmured.

His lips brushed my skin as he spoke, and my hands clutched his shoulders.

"If Minerva hadn't been able to find you, I don't know what would have happened."

He pulled his head away from my throat, looking down at me. He no longer looked angry. His expression was pained. Tortured.

"I don't think I can live without you," he said, his words little more than a rumble.

My heart rate picked up and my nipples pricked. He was looking at me like he wanted to devour me. Like he would never, ever let me go.

He lowered his head until our lips were barely touching.

"You were an unexpected blessing," he continued. "I couldn't have created a woman more perfect for me."

I shuddered against him. He was telling me the truth. The magic inside me insisted it was all true. And not only that, but that he was perfect for me.

His mouth opened over mine, his tongue gliding along my lower lip before he dipped it into my mouth. I clutched at him, trying to pull myself closer.

His arms shifted to my waist, lifting me off my feet. I wrapped my legs around his hips as he carried me out of the bathroom, our mouths fused together.

Garrett crawled onto the bed, using one arm to hold me to him. He lowered me to the mattress, his weight coming down on top of me.

He released me just long enough to jerk his shirt over his head, revealing his hard torso. When he stretched out over me, our bare skin touched, and I sucked in a sharp breath at the sensation. His body emanated heat like a furnace. I ran my hands down his back, digging my fingers into the thick muscles running from his shoulders to his waist.

Garrett's head nudged mine to the side and he nipped at my neck, just hard enough to sting before his lips followed the same path.

My legs locked around his hips as his mouth went lower, tracing a path over my collarbone and down my chest.

Garrett took my nipple in his mouth, sucking deep, and my back arched. My hands fisted in his hair when his lips moved to my other nipple. My body was heating up, my skin soaking up the warmth of his flesh against mine.

I released his hair, wedging a hand between us, and reached down until my fingers brushed the waistband of his shorts.

Garrett released my breast. "Sela—"

My hand slid behind the elastic waistband of his athletic shorts and closed around his length.

Garrett stiffened over me. "Fuck."

"Yes," I said, putting my lips to his pectoral. "We should do that right now."

A hoarse chuckle escaped his throat as I gave his cock an experimental stroke. God, he was long and thick.

I straightened my left leg, lifted myself in a bridge with my right, and shoved him to the side. Garrett didn't resist. He rolled over so that I straddled his hips while his back was to the bed.

"I think it's my turn to touch you this time," I murmured, studying his bare chest and abdomen with a great deal of interest.

"I'm all yours," he said, his hands resting on my hips.

I traced my fingers through the hair on his chest, following the trail lower to his stomach. His abs tightened as I scooted back and grabbed the waistband of his shorts.

I pulled it back, revealing his cock. As I worked the shorts down his hips, his erection bobbed. I tossed the shorts over my shoulder and took in the sight before me.

I'd caught glimpses of Garrett naked before, but not when he was hard and staring at me as though he were biding his time for the perfect moment to pounce.

"Sit up," I murmured, my gaze moving up his body until it reached his face.

Garrett lifted his upper body, his shoulders resting against the padded headboard, and spread his thighs. I crawled between his legs and reached out to wrap my hand around his cock.

His hands fisted on his thighs as I gave him another stroke. I wondered how he would taste.

As I leaned forward, he inhaled, the muscles in his chest and abs tightening.

I licked his tip, humming at the warm, salty taste of his skin. When I opened my mouth and took the tip inside, he groaned.

I swirled my tongue around the tip, pumping his length with my hand. His thighs jerked on each side of me as I took him deeper.

"Sela," he growled.

I looked up at him, lifting my head until only the very tip of his cock was in my mouth.

"I'm barely in control," he panted, his hands moving to clasp the bun on my crown.

I took my mouth off him long enough to ask, "And?"

Then, I took him as deep as I could, moaning when his cock jumped in my mouth.

His hands released my hair, and he grabbed me around my ribs, hauling me up his body. All the air left my body as he moved his hands down to my hips, lifting me to my feet until I was standing right over him, my pussy over his face.

His fingers clamped over my ass, jerking me into his face, and his lips closed around my clit, sucking hard. I cried out, leaning over to rest my palms on the top edge of the headboard. As he sucked my clit, he flicked it with his tongue, driving me toward climax faster than I'd ever experienced before. My legs nearly gave out, but his hands held me over his face, taking most of my weight.

My body jerked and spasmed as the tension coiled within me. A few moments later, I threw my head back and moaned as the orgasm crashed through me. I couldn't hold my body up any longer and I leaned forward until the side of my face pressed against the wall.

As the twitches of my body calmed, Garrett used his grip on my ass to lower me until I straddled his thighs. I looked at him with heavy eyes.

"What was that?"

His only answer was to wipe his face, dragging his fingers through his mouth, and lower it to his cock. I watched as he spread the wetness over his tip. He urged me up on my knees, tilting my hips until he lined up with my entrance. He urged me to lower my body and the tip of his cock slid inside me.

I gasped as he pulled my hips further down, then lifted me up. He did this over and over. I took him in a bit at a time until my ass finally came to rest on his thighs. I trembled over him, my muscles flexing around his girth. I squirmed, trying to get used to the sensation of being so full.

Garrett's eyes were blue-green fire as he looked down to where we were joined. "Are you okay?" he asked.

"Yes," I whispered, shifting my hips again.

I lifted up a few inches before I sank down once more. Garrett hissed and my head fell back as I moaned.

"Look at you taking my cock," he murmured, his eyes still locked between my legs.

I moved again, more this time. His hands clenched around my hips, tilting them at a different angle. I shivered, my pussy tightening at the feel of him rubbing inside me.

"Fuck," he rumbled.

"We are," I sighed, setting a slow, languid rhythm with my hips.

He was hitting spots inside me that I'd never felt before. Garrett leaned over, closing his lips around my nipple again. His teeth caught the tip, tugging lightly.

My body clenched again, and I shuddered over him.

Garrett's hands urged me to move faster, pulling me into him so that his cock went deeper inside me.

That tension gathered between my legs again, ratcheting tighter and tighter until I was teetering on the edge of another orgasm. This one felt so much deeper, larger, than the last. I gasped and panted as my hips jerked in his grip.

"Garrett," I whimpered. "I'm—"

I couldn't finish the words. The breath caught in my throat as he shoved me down on his dick and used his grip on my hips to grind me against him.

"Come on my cock, Sela. I want to feel it."

My hands fisted in his hair again and jerked his head back. Something inside me was shivering...cracking. I sank my teeth into his neck as the orgasm crested and imploded.

In a burst, the black threads binding my soul, the center of my magic, snapped.

I screamed as pleasure and power washed through me and blew through the room.

Garrett groaned, his hands slamming me down on his cock one last time. I felt him then, deep inside me. Not just his cock, but his soul.

He was my mate. My magic recognized him. Wanted him.

We writhed together, both of us trapped in a storm of magic and ecstasy.

As both began to subside, I collapsed against his chest, resting my cheek on his shoulder. Garrett's arms wrapped around me, cradling me closer.

"You bit me," he murmured into my ear.

"Did I hurt you?"

"Never," he answered. "But I'm yours now."

I lifted my head up and looked into his eyes. They were wild again and I realized I was talking to his wolf.

"Are you?"

"Forever," he growled, leaning forward to press his nose against my throat.

My heart sang at the word, but a sliver of fear pierced the center.

Forever was more than enough time for him to grow to hate me as much as he once loved me.

Chapter Eighteen

The spaghetti sauce was scorched, and the pasta had boiled nearly dry, turning the noodles into something resembling dried glue.

Garrett dumped it all in the trash and made us sandwiches. He'd lit a fire in the fireplace in the living room and we cuddled together on a bed of cushions and blankets that he'd dragged out of a closet in the hall.

When my magic burst free, the bedroom had been thrown into disarray. There were broken picture frames on the floor and change scattered everywhere. Garrett insisted I lie on the bed while he cleaned it up. As I'd watched him, my magic hummed inside me. It was a strange feeling, but it was also...right.

Now that we were in the living room, I sipped a fresh vodka and soda since the ice in the first one he'd made me melted down, ruining the drink.

Garrett drank whiskey while he ran his hand up and down my thigh and calf. We were lying in front of the fire, Garrett behind me. I had my top leg crooked and resting over a pillow. My back still hurt from spending a couple hours tied to a stone slab.

Garrett had spread antibiotic ointment on my back after I took a quick shower. Even though I'd taken a bath before, I definitely needed to clean up again once he was done with me.

Now, I wore one of his old flannel shirts. It had been washed so many times that it was incredibly soft.

Since we'd left the bedroom, he'd been touching me every chance he got. His hands brushed my hair, my shoulders. He put an arm around me or pressed his lips to the nape of my neck.

I felt...treasured.

Of course, I had to go and fuck it all up.

"Garrett?" I asked, staring at the fire.

"Yes." His nose nuzzled my hair.

"What happens if mates are unhappy? Are they stuck together?"

His body stiffened behind me. "What?"

I turned over so I could see his face. "I'm asking because of Leona. The way she talked about her mate..." I trailed off, thinking of the best way to put my next thought into words. "She talked about him like she hates him. But they're fated. When I asked Minerva about it earlier, before I was, uh, taken, she said it does happen sometimes. That mates aren't always compatible in personality, even if they are physically."

"Why are you asking about this?" he asked.

"Because I need to know. If I'm going to be your mate, I need to understand. If things aren't working out between us, am I just stuck here? I mean, it doesn't sound like divorce is an option."

He stared down at me. Pain stabbed me in the heart, and I frowned, rubbing a hand over the center of my chest. That was strange.

"If you're going to be my mate?" he asked. The question was little more than a coherent growl.

"Yes. If I'm going to be your mate, I need to understand."

His eyes grew hot, and he sat up, looming over me and bracing his weight on his arms. "Have you forgotten that you bit me. We are mates. You claimed me, Sela. There's no 'if' here."

I gaped up at him. "What?"

He shoved himself away, leaping to his feet. He was still naked. Apparently, shifters didn't have a modest bone in their bodies.

"You claimed me!" he roared. "And now you're asking me about divorce?"

"That's not—"

His eyes locked on mine, and I knew there was no use talking anymore. His wolf was firmly in control. He looked feral. On the edge of shifting.

My legs were shaky as I got to my feet. "Garrett, please. I'm not rejecting you."

It was too late though. His wolf had taken over. He stormed over to the front door and ran outside, slamming it behind him. I stared after him for a split second, at a complete loss. Then, I scrambled after him.

This was just a huge misunderstanding.

I ran outside just in time to see his wolf shake himself and sprint into the woods, faster than I could ever hope to follow.

The entire time, my chest ached as though I'd been stabbed in the heart.

* * *

I waited all night for Garrett to return. I spent almost half that time crying uncontrollably. I hadn't meant to hurt him or anger him. I only wanted reassurance that my fear was unfounded. Instead, he only reinforced that my worries weren't as trivial as I'd hoped.

When he didn't come back, I finally gave up and called Cari for a ride at dawn.

I had to go home. I didn't have any clothes here, or a phone charger. Garrett used a different brand of phone than I did, so I worried I'd be trapped out here with no way to contact anyone.

I'd go to the cottage, shower, get some sleep and food, and then try to find him and talk to him when he was calmer.

I rubbed my sternum as Cari drove me back to the cottage. She'd tried to talk to me when she picked me up, but I just shook my head and told her I couldn't talk about it now.

She stayed, making me a bagel and some scrambled eggs while I showered again. We drank coffee together in the kitchen. She tried to talk to me, but I was too numb to respond.

"He'll come back," she finally said.

I looked up at her where I'd been shredding half my bagel between my fingers. "What?"

"Garrett will come back. He's a good man. He might have gotten upset over something, but he didn't walk away from you. I promise."

I shrugged. "I'm pretty sure I hurt his feelings. Not just a little, but a lot."

"He's a tough guy. He'll get over it and then come talk to you."

I met her gaze. "I'm not so sure he'll want to."

"Sela—" she began.

"I can't talk about it more than that, Cari," I said, my voice breaking over the words. "If I do, I'll break down. I can't break down right now."

"Okay," she sighed. "I have to go open the store."

She got up from the table and came around to hug me.

"Call me if you need me," she said.

I leaned my head against her chest. She was standing beside my chair, her arms wrapped around my shoulders.

"I will," I lied.

She kissed the top of my head. "We'll discuss the whole mates things when you're not so upset," she said. "I still can't believe you didn't tell me."

"I wasn't sure how I felt."

Cari gave me one more squeeze. "Completely understandable. I won't push, but you do need to talk about it at some point."

The sob didn't escape my mouth until the front door shut behind her.

After my crying jag, I managed to take a short nap. When I woke up, I tried to call Garrett. It rang for a long time before it went to voicemail.

I cried again, until my eyes were so swollen that I could barely see.

An hour later, I tried to call him again.

This time, it went straight to voicemail.

He was screening my calls.

I nearly threw my phone across the room. The ache in my chest only deepened then, dragging me down into despair.

This was exactly what I'd been worried about. That I would be trapped and miserable.

I didn't try to call him again. Instead, I went back to bed and escaped into sleep.

Chapter Nineteen

The sun was shining through the bedroom windows when I woke. The light was bright and hurt my sore eyes. They still felt swollen and damp.

I blinked several times before I realized I'd forgotten to close the shades the night before. It had to be the middle of the day based on the amount of light pouring through the windows.

I groaned, rolling over to pick up my phone. It was nearly noon.

As soon as I'd moved, I realized I needed to pee in the worst way. I rolled to my feet, wincing at the soreness in my back and legs. I hobbled to the bathroom, pressing a hand to my lower back.

When I finished, I staggered to the sink to wash my hands and caught a glimpse of myself in the mirror. I looked terrible. My skin was wan and washed out. Dark circles ringed my puffy, bloodshot eyes.

I looked like I was ill.

Or grieving the death of a loved one.

I took a deep breath and decided to pull myself together. I had to figure out what I needed to do next.

I brushed my hair, pulling it back into a ponytail. It was a riot of wild curls from sleeping on it while it was wet. Then, I washed my face with cool water and brushed my teeth.

My legs weren't as stiff as I walked back into the bedroom and grabbed a pair of black joggers and a white sweatshirt. As I got dressed, I thought about my next move.

My first instinct was to leave Devil Springs, but just the thought made the ache in my chest flare into a pain that took my breath away.

Okay, that wasn't an option. Garrett hadn't been lying when he said I'd claimed him. I could still feel him in my soul. If I concentrated hard enough, I could get a split-second glimpse of his emotions. After the first try, I stopped. I couldn't stand the hurt I was sensing.

A hurt I'd inadvertently caused.

Not to mention the fact I'd vowed not to leave until I'd told him or Daniel. Granted, I could get around that by telling Daniel and not him, but it didn't feel right.

I looked over at my phone, yearning to reach out to him again.

But I didn't. He wasn't ready to talk to me.

And, honestly, I wasn't ready to talk to him either. I was hurting, too. I'd wanted reassurance only to end up having him abandon me.

If I couldn't talk to Garrett, I needed to talk to someone. Cari had always been my go-to person when things weren't going well, but she was as human as I was. Or had always thought I was. She didn't understand the intricacies of mates either. Not yet. She and Daniel had only been together for a couple of months.

Then, I thought of Minerva. Maybe she could tell me what I needed to know. Or give me advice on how to handle the situation. She didn't look very old, but she seemed wiser than any other woman I'd ever met.

My course of action decided, I grabbed my phone and wallet, leaving my bag at the cottage. The strap was broken, and I didn't have another one with me. Maybe I could pick one up today.

I didn't bother with my car. The air was cool, but the sun was warm, so a walk in the fresh air sounded like a good idea.

It wasn't until I crossed the square that I started to shake. I'd been so consumed with my own personal angst I hadn't given a thought to the fact that I was kidnapped off this very street just a day ago.

I was breathing heavily by the time I entered Minerva's shop. She came from the back of the store, her eyes wide.

"Sela, what's wrong?"

She hurried around the counter and headed toward me.

"I'm okay," I answered, the words barely coming from my lips. "Just freaking out."

"Why? Did Leona or Edgar try to grab you again?"

I shook my head.

She all but carried me to a stool behind her counter, which was a feat in and of itself. I probably outweighed her by thirty pounds.

I slumped on the stool.

Minerva shuffled around me and grabbed a bottle of water out of a mini fridge below the counter. She cracked the lid and brought it over to me.

"Here. Drink some water."

I took the bottle in shaky hands, lifting it to my mouth. Cool water washed the dryness from my lips. I took another sip.

My heart slowed as I continued to drink.

"I'm sorry," I told her. "I started to freak out when I crossed the square. All I could think about was an SUV pulling in front of me and two big guys jumping out to grab me."

"It's only natural," Minerva said. "It happened yesterday."

She studied me. "You've been crying. Oh, Sela."

I released a watery laugh. "I wasn't crying about the whole kidnapping thing. I was crying about my..." I took another breath. "I was crying about my mate."

"Your mate?" Minerva asked. She started to smile until my face crumpled. "Oh, my goddess, what's wrong? Did something happen?"

"Garrett and I had sex and my magic broke loose...and I bit him. He said that I claimed him. I was happy, but also scared. So then I asked him what happened if mates weren't happy with each other since divorce doesn't seem to be an option and he got all pissed off and stormed out."

Her eyebrows lifted as she looked at me. "Since I last saw you?"

"Yes." Tears crowded my throat, so I drank another mouthful of water.

"Oh, my," she said. Her eyes sparkled. "Well, first of all, I'm so happy to hear that your power is unbound."

"But I screwed up so badly, Minerva. And I didn't even mean to. I was just asking him questions because of some things Leona said while she had me tied to that damn altar." I looked up at Minerva. "She hates her mate. Did you know that?"

Minerva shook her head.

"She as much as said so yesterday. Yet they're stuck with each other. And, honestly, I feel worse for her mate than her because she's obviously a real piece of work, but it also makes me wonder if that's why she became such a raging bitch. I only wanted to know more about it and Garrett said several times I could ask him anything I wanted to know about shifters and mates, so I did."

I couldn't hold back the tears this time. "And he got mad, shifted into a wolf, and ran away. I tried to call him, but he sent my last call to voicemail after the first ring."

"Oh, Sela, I'm so sorry."

I straightened before she could hug me. "I'm starting to get mad though because he made me hopeful that things would work out and now, he's acting like an asshole!"

Minerva nodded. "I understand why you're angry. He's not exactly being fair in this situation."

Before I could say anything else, the door to the store opened and a couple walked in. They were both young and smiling.

I turned my back to them. Minerva waved, clearly familiar with them.

"I'll be right with you," she called. She looked down at me, her bright gold eyes warm and kind. "You sit right here and drink your water. We'll finish our discussion in a few moments."

I nodded because I wasn't ready to walk out of her store anyway. The idea of going back out on the sidewalk made my palms sweat.

Minerva gave my shoulder a pat and walked around the counter, speaking to the couple. I glanced over my shoulder and noticed that the man leaned down to rub his cheek over the woman's. He was scent marking her.

They must be shifters. I blinked and my magic thrummed in my chest. I could see the bond between them. They glowed with the same light.

I watched as Minerva helped them find what they needed. I moved back to the hall behind the counter when they came up to pay.

After they left, Minerva found me in the reading room, sipping water and studying the wallpaper.

"Are you feeling better?" she asked.

I faced her, nodding.

"Ready to continue our chat?"

Chat, as though I hadn't been crying my eyes out a few minutes ago.

I laughed. "Yeah. I have some questions if you don't mind answering them."

"Of course not. I so rarely get to mentor new witches. Come out into the shop. We'll talk while I tidy the counter."

I followed her out and settled back on the stool. I watched as she took a dust rag and wood polish off a small shelf against the wall. She began wiping down the antique wooden counter.

"Those people that just came in. Were they mates?"

Minerva smiled at me. "Yes. They're part of Garrett's pack, in fact."

I nodded. "They're very young."

"They are, but not as young as they look," she said. She kept polishing, letting me come to the point at my own pace.

"They also seemed to be in love."

Minerva's smile widened. "They are. Very much so."

"Do you know how long they've been together?"

"Five years."

I hesitated before I asked my next question. "Is that what mates are usually like?"

Her kind eyes came back to me. "Yes, it is."

"But Leona hates her mate. And you said that sometimes mates aren't compatible in personality, even if they're compatible physically."

Minerva stopped polishing and gave me her complete attention.

"That's true. But I also said it's rare. Most of the time, mates make a great deal of effort to make each other happy. It's instinctive. Especially amongst the shifters. They tend to nurture and care for each other when they're mated."

"What happens if that doesn't work?"

"I've only heard of that happening a few times in the past hundred years or so. If a mated pair just can't get along, they will separate. Usually by a few hundred to a thousand miles."

"That's all."

Minerva nodded. "That's all, but it's not simple. There's pain involved when mates separate. I've heard them describe it as a gnawing ache."

That explained the pain in my chest that hadn't faded since Garrett ran away from me yesterday.

"Do you have any more questions?" Minerva asked.

"Not about mating," I answered, my mind spinning. Now that I had more information, I needed to decide what to do.

"Then what would you like to know?"

Minerva went back to polishing the counter.

"I released my power last night and I need someone to teach me how to use it. Safely. I can feel it inside me. Almost as though it's waiting to be used."

"You mentioned that your power was free." Her smile was sweet, as though she was genuinely happy that I'd come into my own power.

"I was wondering if you would be willing to do it."

She looked up at me, her eyes sparkling like topaz gems. "You want me to teach you?"

"Yes."

She squealed and threw the dust rag down, coming around the counter to throw her arms around me.

"Of course, I'll teach you!" she said, hugging me to her chest and swaying back and forth. "I've always wanted a protégé!"

"Minerva, you're my age. I'm not sure I qualify as a protégé."

She released me. "That's sweet. But I'm nearly ten years older than you, Sela."

I blinked at her. "No way."

She nodded.

I studied her smooth skin. "Then, you need to teach me your skincare routine as well."

She laughed. "Of course."

We were smiling at each other when the front door of the shop opened again, the bell above it tinkling.

I glanced over and my spine went rigid.

Garrett stood just inside the door, clad in a white t-shirt and a pair of faded jeans that were getting ragged at the hems. He looked beautiful to me.

Pain and anger shot straight through my heart as we stared at each other.

Chapter Twenty

My first instinct was to run to Garrett. To leap onto him, wrapping him up with my arms and legs.

My second instinct was to grab the closest item and throw it at his head.

Because these two urges were so strong and opposing, I couldn't move. I stood, frozen to the floor, and stared at him.

The near constant pain that had rested in my chest dissipated.

But it wasn't until Garrett took a step forward that my paralysis was broken. I shook my head.

"What are you doing here?" I asked him.

"I came to talk to you."

He kept walking until he was only a few feet away from me. Up close, in the bright light of day, I could see the purple beneath his eyes and the pallor of his skin. He looked like shit.

A small, petty part of me was glad he was suffering because I'd been suffering, too.

"I tried to talk to you yesterday. More than once," I retorted.

He winced. "I know. I have a lot to apologize for."

That wasn't what I was expecting. "What?"

The door opened again, the bell chiming, and two women came in.

I knew they were witches just by looking at them. Their power shimmered around them like an aura.

Minerva's eyes widened and she took my arm.

"Why don't you two go into the reading room to discuss this?"

She tugged me back to the reading room and basically shoved me inside. Garrett followed. The door snapped shut behind us, leaving us in the dark room.

"Uh, Minerva, we need light."

She didn't answer but all the candles in the room flared to life at once.

"Whoa. That's freaky," I whispered.

I moved around the room, making sure to keep Garrett on the other side.

He stood still, staring at me. His facial expressions were always hard to read. Hell, the man barely smiled.

However, everything he was feeling was written on his face. He looked tortured. And sad.

"You said you wanted to talk," I prompted when he stayed silent, staring at me.

"I did." He cleared his throat. "I mean, I do."

Still, he didn't say anything else.

"Garrett, if you aren't going to speak, then there's nothing else to say."

He sidestepped until his body was in front of the door. I huffed out a harsh laugh.

"I'm sorry, Sela," he said. "I am so damn sorry that I can't even find the words to explain it."

My anger and hurt faded a bit. But only a bit. I kept watching him, waiting. An apology that consisted of a single sentence wasn't going to do the trick.

"I fucked up," he continued. "You were asking me questions, just like I told you I wanted. But you'd just claimed me. My wolf was close to the surface because he thought we should claim you in return. It was only right. I was trying to calm him, explain that you didn't know anything about mates or even what you'd just done. Then, you started talking about being unhappy, about how mates couldn't divorce, and I couldn't control him any longer. He was hurt and angry."

Garrett stopped talking and shook his head.

"That's not entirely true either. I was hurt and angry, too. That's why I couldn't stop him from taking over. He ran away because I forced him to. If I'd stayed, he would have bitten you. Marked you and made you ours. Whether you were willing or not."

The tightness in my chest loosened even more.

"And you hadn't agreed to be ours yet," he continued. Now that the dam was broken, it seemed as though he wasn't going to stop talking until he had it all out. "So, I left the house before the wolf could do something unforgivable."

"I waited for you," I interrupted. "All night."

"I know." The words were raspy. "I lose time when I'm in an... emotional state. The wolf takes over and I don't even realize how long I've been—" He shook his head again. "I'm sorry, Sela."

"I called you twice in the last twelve hours, too," I said. "You didn't answer or call me back the first time and then you sent me to voicemail the second time."

"I know. I'm sorry for that, too. I was still in the forest when you called the first time. And the second..." He paused. "I knew that I needed to see you face-to-face. To apologize in person. It was the right thing to do. Once I was calm enough to control the wolf, I cleaned up and came to find you."

My guard was still up, but I felt the need to explain.

"Garrett, you need to know. I wasn't asking those questions because I'm unhappy with the idea of being your mate. But I am worried about the future. This is all completely new to me, and it seems crazy to think that two complete strangers could be happy together for the rest of their lives just because they're 'destined' for each other." I paused, gathering my thoughts. "And Leona said some things while she had me. She's miserable with her mate. In fact, that's one reason why she wants to wake the blood god. She seems to think he has the power to break mate bonds and that's what she wants. She wants to be rid of her mate. For good."

I didn't mention her egotistical trip over how she thought supernaturals should be in charge of the world. I was certain that Daniel's head would explode when he found out that little tidbit.

Garrett rubbed his hands over his face.

"Nathaniel tried everything to make Leona happy, but she's the kind of person who could have everything on her wish list and still find it wanting. She's never satisfied with anything. Not even herself. That's why she's determined to break the mate bond. And it does happen. Sometimes people don't want to be mated or aren't willing to work together to make their lives peaceful. But that's extremely rare because our animals push us to make our mates happy. To take care of them, feed them, touch them. It's not just a desire to fulfill our mate's needs. It's a drive. An uncontrollable impulse. I should have explained all this to you before, but—" He stopped speaking. He'd already told me why.

"So, what now?" I asked.

"Please give me a chance to make this right," he said. "To show you that I can be the kind of mate you want."

That was the thing. He'd already proven that he was the kind of mate I would want. Yes, he'd reacted poorly when I hurt his feelings, but now I realized the pain I'd felt that night was his, not mine. The pain in my chest this entire time hadn't just been because we were separated, but because he was hurting.

It was still there, weaker now, but there was still an ache nonetheless.

"You don't need a chance," I said with a sigh. "I realized when I saw you today, that you are what I need. It scares me a little considering I've known you for less than a week, but you've already proven to me that you have my back. That'll you'll show up when I need you. And that you're willing to admit your mistakes and try to fix them. That's more than anyone else has ever given me before, except for Cari. And I can't marry Cari because she's too much like a sister rather than a wife."

"What are you saying?" he asked, his body tense.

"I'm saying that I accept you as my mate. I don't want to know what it's like to live without you in my life."

His eyes brightened and his body seemed to swell.

A moment later, he came around the table, taking my arms in his hands.

"Are you certain?" he asked, a growl edging his voice. "Because if I claim you, I will never be able to let you go. Never." He stopped. "I'm lying. It's already too late. I was planning to do whatever it took to get you to accept me. Even if I had to handcuff you to my bed like Daniel did with Cari."

"Daniel did what?" I asked, my brain catching on his last words.

"Later. Answer me. Are you sure this is what you want? That I'm what you want?"

"I'm sure."

In a blink, Garrett scooped me up in his arms and headed out the door.

He rushed past Minerva, who was now alone in the store again.

"I'll talk to you tomorrow, Sela!" she called, waving as we passed. A golden glow flowed from her hand, catching me around my left forearm where the burn was still pink and shiny.

I wondered if she was healing it again.

"Next week," Garrett growled.

Minerva laughed, the light, silvery sound following us out onto the street.

Garrett ran through the square, ignoring the way people stopped to watch us as we passed.

"Where are we going?" I asked.

"Your cottage. It's closer."

"Closer for what?"

He glanced down at me, his eyes glowing with aquamarine fire.

My body heated and his steps sped up until he was nearly sprinting.

He reached the sidewalk in front of the cottage and pounded up the concrete and the porch steps. I laughed when he tried to turn the knob and it wouldn't move.

"It's locked. Hang on."

I dug my keys out of the side pocket of my leggings. Garrett set me down while I fitted the key into the lock. My hands were shaking with excitement and anticipation.

And maybe a little bit of nerves.

Finally, the knob turned beneath my hand and Garrett crowded me through the door. I moved to the table in the front hall and dropped my keys and wallet on it before I turned to face him.

Garrett reached behind him, shutting the door, and locking it. I backed up a few more steps, keeping my eyes on him.

"Where are you going?" he growled, lowering his head. "Come here."

I shook my head, smiling a little. "I don't think so."

"Sela, I'm not fully in control here."

"I know," I answered, my smile growing.

I reached down and tugged my sweatshirt over my head, tossing it to the side, still backing up toward the stairs.

"Where are you going?" he asked, stalking after me.

Without answering, I whirled and rushed up the steps, running as fast as I could. Which was pretty fast when I put some effort into it.

I'd just reached the top step when two strong arms wrapped around me. I laughed and relaxed into his grip when he hauled me through the door to my bedroom. Garrett pushed me down onto the bed before he backed up to shut the door and lock it.

I pushed myself up onto my elbows and looked down my body at him. "Worried we'll be interrupted?"

"I'm not taking any chances," he snarled, ripping his shirt over his head.

I managed to kick off my sneakers and take off my socks when he appeared in front of me, his hands on his belt. He pulled it out of the beltloops on his jeans with a hiss, but stopped when I leaned back and lifted my hips to shimmy out of my leggings.

"What are you waiting for?" I asked, unhooking my bra, and tossing it to the side.

When my thumbs went to the waistband of my panties, he sprang into action. He unbuttoned and unzipped his jeans, shoving them down his legs.

I was naked and lounging on the pillows at the head of the bed by the time he removed his shoes, socks, and pants.

Garrett crawled up the bed until he was hovering over my body.

"Last chance to change your mind," he rumbled.

I hooked a hand on the back of his neck and tugged him in for a kiss. Our lips clashed and our tongues tangled.

I moaned at the taste of him. Garrett lowered his weight over me, pressing our bodies together. He was so hot. I wrapped my arms and legs around him, trying to pull him as close as possible.

It had only been a little over a day since the last time I saw him, but I'd missed him. I'd missed his presence. His touch.

Garrett's hands were all over me, cupping my breasts, kneading my ass, and dipping between my legs to skate over my clit. My skin was buzzing at his touch, and I dug my nails into his back.

I needed more. I needed his cock inside me, deep and hard. I needed his bite.

"Garrett, I want—"

His mouth moved down my throat and chest until he reached my nipple. He licked and sucked, closing the edge of his teeth around the tip. The pleasure that arced through me bordered on pain with its intensity.

"Inside me," I panted. "I need you inside me."

Garrett levered himself up. He grabbed my hips and flipped me over onto my belly. I gasped at the sudden move but followed the urging of his hands when he pulled me up onto my knees. His hand came around to cup my pussy, his fingers circling my clit in firm circles. Air escaped my lungs on a rush when two fingers of his other hand entered me from behind.

My body clenched down on him, but it wasn't enough.

"Your cock," I demanded. "I want it."

Garrett growled, but his hands left my pussy. He gripped my ass, spreading me, and I knew he was looking at my pussy. I shuddered when one of his thumbs skated over my entrance up to my asshole, pressing against it briefly.

Jesus, he was driving me insane.

"Garrett!"

He laughed, but it was a sound I hadn't heard before. It was raspy and deep.

"Little witch wants my cock?" he snarled.

A rush of fire speared through me. This wasn't Garrett. Not completely. It was his wolf.

"Yes," I answered.

186

He leaned over my back, resting his weight on one hand. His dick nudged my pussy, the tip prodding me but never entering me.

"And my bite?" he whispered, his teeth closing around my shoulder. They were sharper than usual. He didn't break the skin, just held me still with his teeth pressing into my flesh.

I shivered at the sensation.

"Yes," I panted.

Garrett growled, releasing my shoulder from his mouth. He shoved himself upright again, one of his hands clamping down on my hip and the other going between us. He used his thumb to spread me apart and then his cock was there. He dipped inside of me, just deep enough to make my body clench around him. Then, he pulled out.

I whimpered, trying to rock my hips back and chase his erection.

A hand came down hard on my ass, making me yelp.

"You take what I give you," he growled.

I snarled back at him, glaring over my shoulder. "Then, give me what I want."

Again, that raspy laugh drifted over my skin. His eyes were wild and burning.

"You're going to get it when I want you to," he said.

His cock was inside me again, this time a little deeper. My arms shook as I tried to hold still.

The wolf taking me growled. "Good little witch."

My body gripped him, trying to keep him inside me. To pull him deeper.

His hand smacked my ass again. "Don't move."

"Then you should make me stay still," I taunted.

His other hand tightened on my hip and the hand that just slapped my ass moved up my spine to grip my hair. My back arched as he tugged and pleasure shot through me, straight to my center.

"Garrett," I whispered. "I need you."

He groaned, still holding me still in front of him, but his hips snapped forward, pushing him deep.

I cried out as he filled me, thrusting hard. My entire body shook with the force of it. This was what I wanted. What I needed.

Garrett slammed inside of me, over and over again, using his grip on my hair and my hip to pull me into his thrusts.

I moaned, my legs trembling as he hit a spot deep inside me, driving my pleasure higher.

The hand at my hip slipped around me, his fingers pressing over my clit. He used quick, firm circles to stroke me, winding my body tighter.

Garrett leaned over me, and I felt his hot breath on the back of my neck. His teeth closed around my shoulder, but he didn't bite down.

He was waiting for something.

I was so close, my body poised to explode. I couldn't do anything but brace myself against the power of his thrusts. His fingers on my clit moved faster and his hips slammed into mine one last time, grinding deep.

I gasped, my back arching up to meet his chest, and my entire body locked down as the orgasm rolled over me and took me under.

The teeth in my shoulder clamped down, breaking through the skin, and I screamed.

Pain and pleasure twisted together. The orgasm swelled again, and my entire body writhed uncontrollably.

Garrett snarled against my skin, his arms banding around my waist to hold me tighter. My body collapsed onto the bed beneath his weight, and he followed me down, grinding his hips against my ass as he drove as deep as possible inside my pussy.

My breath was coming in gasps as the climax began to recede. My hips twitched as my body spasmed from aftershocks, clenching around his dick.

Garrett's mouth released my shoulder, and I felt his lips and tongue move over the bite.

The feeling inside my chest swelled, moving outward and into Garrett. His breath stuttered as my magic met his, twisting together.

His hips moved and we both moaned.

"I feel you," he murmured. The rasp was gone from his voice. The wolf must have retreated.

"I feel you, too."

"Then, you know."

I turned my head, but I couldn't see him. "Know what?"

He turned me onto my side so I could see him, but he was still inside me. "That I love you."

I hesitated, touching the bond between us with my magic. I felt it then. The warmth of his love. It burned inside him like a smoldering coal.

"Yes, I feel it," I said.

His lips nuzzled my shoulder then my cheek.

"And you love me," he whispered.

There was no denying it now. He could feel it as clearly as I could. The time for fear had passed.

"I do."

He smiled down at me. "Then you don't have to worry."

"About what?"

"That things won't work out between us. As long as that love remains, we will figure it out. Always."

I tilted my head so I could press my lips against his. And the fragile hope inside me bloomed into joy.

Because he was right.

If we put that love first, we could face anything. Together.

Chapter Twenty-One

Garrett and I were snuggled up in the bed, both of us still naked. He was propped up on the pillows and I was cradled between his legs, my chest against his and my cheek against his shoulder.

The fingers of one of his hands threaded through my hair, making my scalp tingle with bliss.

His other hand stroked my shoulder and arm.

I felt cherished. Not just because of the way he touched me, but because of the feelings of love and affection that drifted through the bond that connected us.

He didn't want to be anywhere other than right here. Maybe forever.

And I agreed.

I sighed against his chest, burrowing my cheek closer so I could hear his heartbeat.

"What do we do now?" I asked.

"Well, I figured I'd finally take you out to Sam and Remi's tonight and then we can come back here and—"

I pinched him, which made him chuckle.

"I'm talking big picture, Garrett."

"I know," he said, cradling me closer.

"I mean, clearly I'm moving here. But I hate the idea of staying in the cottage while you live in your house," I said.

He stilled. "What are you saying?"

I lifted my head to look into his eyes. "How do you feel about having a roommate? But I'd have to sleep in your bed."

The hand stroking my hair fisted the strands and pulled me toward his lips.

When he released my mouth, we were both breathing hard again, and his cock was swelling against my hip.

"That's a yes?" I asked.

"Yes," he growled.

I smiled. "And you have to marry me."

His pupils expanded. "What?"

"I know the mates thing is a big deal among supernatural beings, but I was raised as a human. I want a wedding. It doesn't have to be big or fancy. Just the people we care about, us, and maybe a pretty white dress and some flowers."

His brows lifted. "Okay."

"And you're going to wear a wedding ring."

He winced at that, and I frowned at him.

"I'd love to, Sela, but I'd lose it the first time I had to shift on the fly."

Okay, that made sense.

I thought for a moment, cocked my head, and asked, "How do you feel about tattoos?"

His arms closed around me, holding me tight, and he released a bark of laughter. "Am I going to have to tattoo your name over my heart?"

"While I really like that idea," I said. "I'd settle for a wedding ring tattoo on your left hand. But you can do both if you want."

Garrett's smile was wide, and his eyes sparkled. I so rarely got to see him like this that I drank in the sight.

"We'll start with the ring tattoo," he said.

"Sounds good."

I lowered my head back to his chest and began tracing a finger over his pectoral muscle.

191

"I hate to bring this up," I said. "But I didn't get a chance to ask earlier. Did your man find Leona and Sommerton?"

Garrett growled. "No. They've basically vanished. Marshall couldn't find any trace of Leona's scent and Sommerton did something to cover his magical trail. Minerva tried to use a spell to find him, but it didn't work. She's pissed as hell. Said she'll do some experimenting and figure it out because he's not going to get away with hurting her protégé."

I sighed. "She called me that?"

Garrett chuckled. "She likes you a lot, Sela. I think you've got a friend there whether you want one or not."

That didn't sound like a bad thing, especially if Leona and Sommerton really thought that they needed me to complete their task.

"Do you think they'll try to get me again?" I asked.

"Maybe, but you'll be living with me, which means you'll be much safer."

Yes, I'd be safer while he was there, but he had to work at some point. What was I going to do then? I definitely needed Minerva to show me the ins and outs of my magic. And for Garrett to teach me how to fight a shifter. Remembering the claws that speared from Leona's fingers in the cavern, I hated the idea of fighting her, but what if I had no other choice?

"Do you know anything about this blood god that they want to release?" I asked, my mind switching gears.

"No," Garrett sighed. "But Minerva probably does. We'll have to talk to her and find out what she knows."

There were so many unanswered questions surrounding what Leona and Sommerton were trying to do. I had a feeling it was going to drive me nuts. Maybe I needed a little distraction. I wiggled against Garrett, feeling his erection poking my hip again. Okay, a big distraction.

I shifted and turned so I could straddle his hips. "We can talk to her tomorrow," I said. "Tonight, I want to celebrate with my mate."

His eyes lit up as he grabbed my ass, rolling his hips so his cock pressed against my clit.

"Or maybe day after tomorrow," I murmured.

Then, I kissed my mate.

* * *

Three days later, Garrett and I parked in front of Minerva's house. I stared at it in awe. It looked almost exactly like the house from the movie about two sisters who were witches. I'd always loved it and wished I could live in a home like it.

"What's wrong?" Garrett asked.

"Nothing. I just...love her house."

He grinned. "Well, just say the word and I'll build you one."

"Maybe when we're ready for kids," I said.

It was Garrett's turn to fall silent. I took advantage of the moment to get out of his vehicle.

He sprang into action as soon as I got out, exiting the driver's seat and coming around the vehicle. "And when would that be?" he asked.

"Maybe in a couple of years," I said.

His fingers laced with mine.

"I'd like some time alone with you first," I said.

He squeezed my hand.

"Plus, I need to understand more about shifters and my power before I start having little half-witch, half-werewolf babies."

He grinned down at me. "That would be a good idea."

The front door of the house opened, and Minerva appeared on the front porch, looking every inch the witch that she was.

"Come in, come in," she said, gesturing for us to go inside. "Everyone else is here."

As soon as I walked into the living room, Cari leapt up from the sofa and threw her arms around me.

I hugged her, a twinge of guilt in my belly. I'd texted her a few times over the last few days, letting her know that Garrett and I had made up, but I hadn't seen her in person.

She released me, looking up at me with a wide grin on her face. "I'm so happy to see you." She gave a little jump. "And you're going to live here! I'll be able to see you all the time!"

She hugged me again and I laughed. "So, you're not mad that I haven't really talked to you in a few days?"

Cari released me completely and backed away. "No, I know what it's like to be newly mated." She glanced at Daniel and there was blush in her cheek.

Okay, more than I needed to know.

"Would you like some tea?" Minerva asked. "Please make yourselves comfortable."

I settled on the other sofa, which faced the one that Daniel and Cari were sitting on.

"No, thanks," I said.

A young woman walked into the living room. She looked a bit like Minerva, the same red hair but it fell in wild curls around her shoulders and she had a similar build, short but curvy. Her eyes were a different color though. A light blue, so pale they were almost grey. Those eyes gave her an ethereal air, as though she could see right through you and into your soul.

My power sensed hers, but it was muted. She was another witch then. I wondered if her magic was bound.

"Aunt Minnie, I got here as fast as I could," she said. "What's the emergency?"

"Daniel, Garrett, Cari...you remember Allison, yes?" Minerva said in response to the woman's question.

They all nodded.

Minerva continued, "Allison, I asked you here because you're in danger."

Allison frowned. "What?"

"Sit, sit," Minerva said, shooing the woman toward a chair next to hers.

Allison did as she requested, settling onto a deep blue chair. "Why do you think I'm in danger?" she asked.

Minerva took a deep breath. "Because your magic is ready to awaken, and there are powers at play that wish to use you for their own ends."

Allison gaped at her aunt. "What are you talking about? I don't have any magic. I'm a null," she murmured, her eyes dropping to where her hands were clasped in her lap.

"I thought you were for a long time," Minerva agreed. "But I was wrong. Your powers have been suppressed, so deeply that even I couldn't sense them. But they're rising now. Enough that I could feel them. Enough that they triggered a premonition."

Allison's head snapped up and she looked at Minerva. "What premonition?"

"Do you remember the myths of the old gods that I told you?" Minerva asked.

Allison nodded.

"The blood god sleeps in the mountain outside of town," Minerva explained. "And you are the key to waking him up."

"Waking him up?" I asked. "I thought he was trapped."

Minerva shook her head. "I thought the blood god was long gone, too," she answered. "Until Leona and Edgar took you. Then, I thought they were right, that he was trapped in the mountain. But he's not. He's sleeping."

"Why is he sleeping?" I asked.

Minerva started to answer, but her niece interrupted.

"How am I the key?" Allison asked, flashing me an apologetic look.

I understood. I'd want to know how I fit into all this, too. More than I'd want to know why the blood god was slumbering beneath the mountain.

"I found a story in one of the old grimoires in the library. I'm assuming Leona found this story as well, but she didn't understand what it meant. The blood god went to sleep long ago, his power drained by his enemies. In the story, which I believe is actually a premonition, when the last of a witch with no magic is awakened, so will he."

Allison shook her head. "That makes no sense. It's a complete contradiction. A witch with no magic is human. And no human has ever awoken with enough power to wake a god. It's never happened in all of the recorded history of witches."

I agreed with Allison. The explanation sounded like an oxymoron.

"I fear what will happen if Leona and Edgar continue to interfere," Minerva continued. "Rather than waking the blood god, they may bring about the destruction of Devil Springs."

"How?" Allison asked.

"If the blood god is woken by the wrong person, his ascent to his full power will decimate the town. It will be like a bomb going off in that mountain. Or a volcano erupting. And it might not just destroy the town. It may destroy the land for many miles outside of this area."

Okay, everyone now looked freaked the hell out.

"I'm sorry to interrupt," Daniel said. "But why are we here? How are we involved?"

Minerva turned to him. "Because I'm going to need your help. Ally will need your help," she answered.

"How?" Garrett asked.

"She needs to be protected. The premonition was very clear about that. If Leona and Edgar realize she is now the key, that Sela is no longer who they need, they will take her. And when they do, they will set a chain of events in motion that will lead to the ruin of this town and the beings in it."

"What chain of events?" Garrett asked.

Minerva took a deep breath. "I can't tell you."

My mate scoffed. "How am I supposed to protect your niece if I don't know what the threat may be or when it's coming?"

The witch sighed. "With premonitions, it's unwise to share too many details with others involved. It alters the outcome and usually not for the better. It would be wrong of me to tell you too much," she said. "It could put you and your mate in danger as well. You two play an important part in this future, but that may change if I let you glimpse even the briefest bit of what may happen."

I could see that Garrett was poised to argue, but I put a hand on his arm.

"She's telling the truth."

He looked down at me, taking in my expression. I'd explained to him how I could always sense if someone was lying to me, so he knew that I was right.

"Fine," he finally relented. But he didn't sound happy. At all.

Daniel was uncharacteristically silent. As the mayor, he tended to jump right into the center of any issues that arose in town. But now, he was listening intently, not speaking.

Minerva turned to him. "You have the Devil's Playground warded," she stated. "I can reinforce the magic to make those wards even more powerful."

Daniel nodded.

"There's more," Minerva continued. "You have a gargoyle on staff there. His resistance to magic and ability to fend off shifter claws and teeth make him an excellent choice to guard Ally. Neither Leona nor Edgar would be able to attack him alone, or even together."

"What?" Allison asked, her voice high.

"Dax Tremaine is my employee. I can't force him to guard Allison," Daniel answered.

"No," Minerva answered. "But you could ask. You know he would do it if you did."

Daniel studied her. "You realize what you're asking, don't you?"

She nodded. "If he requires more payment, I am happy—"

Daniel silenced her with a lift of his hand. "You know he won't require financial payment. But there will be a cost."

"I know," Minerva said.

Hey!" Allison interrupted. "Can the two of you not talk about me as though I'm not in this room and I don't have a say?"

Minerva got to her feet and moved to kneel in front of Allison, taking both of her hands in hers. "You have to remain safe," she said. "I promised your parents that I would love you and protect you as though you were my own. I couldn't adore you more if I'd carried you in my own body and birthed you myself. I am telling you that you're in danger and begging you to do what I ask." Minerva's voice broke for a moment. She swallowed and continued. "I couldn't bear if anything happened to you. You are the light of my life, Ally. Please listen to me and do what I ask."

Allison looked at her for a long moment before her shoulders slumped. "Very well."

Daniel got to his feet, pulling his phone out of his pocket. "I'll call Dax."

He looked at Garrett and my mate got to his feet.

"I'll be right back," Garrett said to me.

At my nod, he left the room with Daniel.

Cari came over to my couch, sitting next to me.

"Minerva, I hate to ask a stupid question," Cari said. "But why are Sela and I here?" she asked.

Minerva released Allison's hands and moved back to her chair. "Because the two of you have a part to play as well," she answered.

Cari shrugged. "But I'm human. What could I have to offer when it comes to shifters, magic, and old gods?"

Minerva smiled. "Every living thing has magic. Even humans. The magic of friendship is more powerful than you realize. You and Sela are close, and with your help, Ally will have everything she needs to fulfill her role."

Okay, that was vague. By the expression on Allison's face, she was used to it. Also, was Minerva basically saying that Cari and I just needed to be friends with Allison in order to help her remain safe?

Before I could ask more questions, Daniel came back into the living room, Garrett trailing behind him.

"Dax is on his way."

For some reason, I felt the compulsion to look at Allison. Her face was pale, and her eyes were wide. She looked equally terrified and excited. I wondered if she had a history with this Dax guy they were talking about.

Garrett came over to the couch, his hand taking mine and pulling me to my feet. One look at his eyes and I realized his wolf was riding him. The mating fever he mentioned was no joke. We'd spent more time in bed than out of it in the last three days.

"Minerva, I need to take my mate home," Garrett rumbled.

A small smile tugged at Minerva's mouth. "Of course." She looked at me. "Call me tomorrow. Garrett has my number. We need to begin your training as soon as possible."

I barely had time to nod before my mate was dragging me out of the house and toward his SUV. Once we were on the road, I said, "You know, no one would probably bother of us if we went out to your cabin for a couple of days."

I laughed as the tires squealed when he jerked the car into a J-turn and headed out of town, toward his property near the mountains.

I was looking forward to having my mate to myself for a day or two. And not having to worry that the neighbors could hear me yelling his name several times a day.

Epilogue

ALLISON

My heart was pounding in my chest as I packed clothes and toiletries in a bag.

Dax Tremaine was on his way here. For me.

My hands shook and I nearly dropped the bras I was pulling out of my dresser.

For years, I'd wondered how it would feel to be waiting for Dax to pick me up. Only, in my daydreams, he was picking me up for a date. Not because I needed protection from a threat that I didn't truly understand.

I'd long since gotten used to Aunt Minnie's premonitions. She saw things that I couldn't and refused to talk about them.

Like the time she forced me to stay home from a party that I'd really wanted to attend in high school. She was more insistent than I'd ever seen her. We had a huge knockdown-drag-out fight about it. I'd been so angry with her.

Then, the next morning, we heard about a single car accident in the same area as the party was being held. On the road I would have taken to come home. A witch had gotten power-drunk from practicing black magic and crashed into a tree. She hadn't survived.

I knew then that my aunt had seen my death in that crash. That was why she'd kept me home. Since that day, I almost never argued with her when she had premonitions and asked me to follow her instructions. I trusted her with my life because she'd probably saved it on more than one occasion.

Now, I was about to go home with the gargoyle I'd had a crush on since I was old enough to understand sexual attraction. The gargoyle I'd secretly been in love with for nearly a decade.

"Ally, Dax is here," she said from the door to my room.

I stuffed a few more things in the bag and zipped it. "I'm ready," I told her.

Aunt Minnie walked over, cupping my face with her hands. It was strange, really. She was only eleven years older than me, but she had taken on the role of my surrogate mother with ease after my parents died.

"Call me every day," she said.

"I will."

"And listen to Dax. He's been a guardian his entire existence. If he tells you to do something, please do it without question. I want you to be safe."

"I will," I answered, barely refraining from rolling my eyes.

She smiled at me, leaning in to kiss my cheek.

"I love you."

I hugged her. "I love you, too."

She released me, her golden eyes gleaming. In that moment, she looked so much like my mother that my heart ached.

"Time to go."

I followed her downstairs, carrying my heavy bag in one hand and my backpack, which held my laptop and purse, slung over my shoulder.

Dax Tremaine stood at the base of the stairs, his huge arms crossed over his chest. His pale skin gleamed in the sunlight streaming in through the windows. His dark brown hair was cut short and close to his scalp on the sides but longer on top. Deep blue eyes that were nearly purple locked on me as I came down.

My knees went weak as I reached the last step and I stumbled. I dropped the bag and landed against a hard chest with an oomph. Two hard hands closed around my biceps, keeping me steady even as my backpack slid down my arm to bang against the back of my legs.

"You okay?" Dax asked, looking down at me with concerned eyes.

My heart raced and a blush rushed to my cheeks because I knew he could probably hear the pounding of my runaway pulse.

"I'm fine," I said, straightening and stepping away. "Thank you."

His gaze tracked me as I slung the weight of the backpack back over my shoulder and went to pick up my bag.

His hand closed over the strap at the same time mine did.

"I've got it," he said, his voice gravelly like the stone he could turn into at will.

My face heated even more. "It's okay—"

He didn't let me finish. His other hand hooked the top loop of my backpack, taking it off my shoulder, and he hefted the duffel bag that held my clothes as though it weighed nothing.

"I've got it," he repeated.

Without another word, he carried them out the door and to the truck parked in front of Aunt Minnie's house.

I glanced at her, feeling hopelessly awkward. She smiled at me, her expression reassuring.

"It will be okay," she said. "Just trust me."

"I do," I told her, blowing out a breath.

It was me I didn't trust. I was nervous enough around Dax the few times I saw him a month. Being around him all the time was going to be much, much worse.

Then again, maybe I would be able to get over this ridiculous crush if I was near him for an extended length of time. Maybe some of his gross habits or personality flaws would come to the fore and I would get over the wild longing that filled me whenever I saw him.

Dax came back to the door and nodded at Minerva. "I'll text when we arrive at the resort." His impassive eyes came to me. "Let's go."

I gave Aunt Minnie one more hug, taking comfort from her lavender and sunshine scent. Then, I followed him out the door into the unknown.

Sign up for my monthly newsletter to read a special bonus epilogue featuring Sela and Garrett! Sela is supposed to meet the pack for the first time, but things don't go according to plan...

Sign up for the Weekly Wood to read the prologue from Garrett's point of view!

Don't Wake the Dead

EXCERPT

Chapter One

If I'd realized he was in the elevator, I wouldn't have stepped inside. I always tried to avoid him, but I wasn't paying attention that morning.

"It's you."

I looked up from my phone and fought not to cringe. Immediately, I returned my attention back to the screen of my phone.

He leaned into me. "Why won't you talk to me?"

Ducking my head, I focused on responding to Jonelle's text as I pretended that he didn't exist.

Suddenly, I felt an icy cold tingle on the side of my face. I jerked away from him, banging my shoulder into the wall. He stood next to me, his tongue hanging out of his mouth like some sort of overgrown puppy.

The other two people in the elevator, a man and a woman, turned and gave me concerned looks. Then they looked at each other as if to say, "You'll help hold her down if she loses her shit, right?"

I smiled wanly. "Sorry, I tripped."

The woman glared at me, but the man eyed me speculatively. I shrugged, trying to look as harmless as possible.

They turned their backs toward me but I could tell that they were on guard. Irritated, I glared at the man to my right. Quickly, I pulled up the note app on my phone and typed him a message.

Leave me alone. And don't ever lick my face again, asshole.

"I just wanted your attention. Why won't you talk to me?" he complained, his voice quieter this time. "You're the only one who seems to see or hear me."

Bcuz I am.

"But why? Why do they all pretend they can't see me?" Now his tone was verging on whiny.

They can't. You know they can't.

"I don't understand. Why can't they see me?"

Usually I tried to be considerate when talking to someone in his position, but we'd had this conversation before. In fact, we'd had this conversation at least once a week since I'd been hired at the insurance firm. If I was alone in the elevator, I would express my annoyance out loud but this time I was hampered by the two other occupants. He knew it too, which was why he was still bothering me. If anything, he was tenacious and willfully ignorant.

I've told u a million times, Jerry. Ur dead. Uve been dead for a long time.

"I can't be dead," he argued.

Sick of arguing with him, I typed him a final message.

U R a ghost. Don't bother me again or I'll come back with holy water and banish ur ass.

Though I wasn't even sure if holy water would work, it seemed like a viable threat. Maybe my words were cruel, but Jerry had been haunting this building daily for the last four years that I worked here. At first, I managed to ignore him, but I made the mistake of responding to his questions once when I was alone. Since then, he tried to talk to me every time he saw me. I was pretty sure he looked for me.

"Bitch," he muttered.

I realized then that not only did Jerry understand that he was dead, he enjoyed being undetectable. He liked moving among the living mostly unseen. The harassment he dished out to me was his way of relieving boredom.

Still, he had no intention of moving on. He wanted to remain here, even if no one else could see or talk to him. Probably so he could look up women's skirts or lick their toes in the elevator, the pervy fucker.

When the elevator reached my floor, I rushed off, accidentally bumping into the woman near the doors.

She huffed in annoyance.

Glancing back, I apologized, "Sorry."

I didn't wait to hear a response from her or Jerry, already hurrying down the hallway toward the offices that held the insurance company that employed me.

The receptionist, Claire, smiled and waved at me as I entered. I nodded to her and headed straight toward the break room where the employee lockers were located. I put my purse inside my locker and took a quick trip to the ladies room. Once I was done, I headed back into the break room for a cup of coffee. It was the same routine I went through every workday morning.

As I added sugar and creamer, my boss, Mike, stuck his head into the break room.

"I need to see you in my office before you start your shift," he stated.

"Okay," I replied.

Before I could ask him if everything was okay, he disappeared. That was a bad sign. Mike might not be the friendliest man I'd ever met, but he never ended conversations so abruptly.

My stomach twisted as I stirred my coffee. I might not be clairvoyant, but I had an idea what was coming. I'd been hearing rumors about company restructuring for a couple of months.

I made my way to Mike's office. I noticed halfway down the hall that I'd left my coffee on the counter in the break room. It didn't matter. I wouldn't have been able to drink a drop right now anyway.

I knocked on his open door and stuck my head in when he called out.

"Hey, Mike."

His face was serious as he gestured for me to come inside. "Please close the door behind you."

That's when I knew my worries were well founded. Mike had a stringent open-door policy in the office. Meetings, unless they were reprimands or terminations, were always held with the door open.

Mike wanted his employees to trust him and refused to hide in his office.

I shut the door and took a seat in the chair across from his. Lacing my fingers together, I rested my hands in my lap and waited.

Mike sighed and mimicked my pose, his expression unhappy. "You're an intelligent person, Zoe, I'm sure you already have an idea of why I called you in here."

"If this has something to do with the rumors of company restructuring, then yes," I answered.

"I'm afraid it does."

"Go ahead and spit it out, Mike," I invited.

"General Insurance is eliminating over a thousand positions this year. All claims centers will pare down from five hundred to four hundred claim reps. As much as I hate this, I have to terminate people based on seniority and you're one of my newer reps."

My eyebrows lifted. "After four years, I'm a newer rep?"

He shrugged. "It's twenty percent of my staff, Zoe. A few of these terminations are for people who've been here longer than you." His face fell. "For what it's worth, I hate doing this and I'm sorry."

"It's okay, Mike," I replied.

Even though it wasn't okay as I claimed, I couldn't be angry with him. He had a job to do, even if he didn't necessarily like it.

I hauled myself out of my chair. "So I take it I have the day off?"

He sighed and I felt a twinge of remorse for my quip. "I've enjoyed working with you. Please put me down as a reference. I'll give any prospective employers a glowing recommendation."

My smile was half-hearted but I appreciated his effort. "Thanks, Mike."

I trudged out of his office, unsure of what to do next. Retracing my steps, I returned to the break room. My full coffee cup was still sitting on the counter. I poured it down the sink and washed the mug.

I didn't bother to go to my cubicle. I stopped bringing personal items to work when I realized that Norma, the woman in the workspace directly behind me, was a kleptomaniac and stole everything on my desk that wasn't nailed down. Except for my work files. Those she was happy to leave.

Removing my bag from my locker, I left the break room and took one last look around the place I'd worked for the last four years. The bland grey carpet and white walls weren't much and the generic landscape paintings hanging throughout the offices were actually damn ugly, but I'd enjoyed my time here.

Now, I was leaving for good.

I said good-bye to Claire as I left. She seemed to know exactly what was going on because she looked sad.

The elevator doors opened up and I was face-to-face with Jerry the Annoying Ghost again. He sneered at me as I stepped on.

"Back so soon?" he asked.

After I pressed the button for the first floor, I faced him. "For the last time. I gotta tell you, Jerry, I won't miss you."

"Miss me?" he asked.

I was actually kind of glad I was alone in the elevator with him so I could speak freely without people thinking I was a fruitcake.

"It's my last day. I won't be back."

He actually looked surprised. "But who'll I talk to?"

I laughed. "No one, Jer. No one. You should really think about moving on."

The elevator steadily descended toward the bottom floor with no stops.

"You can't leave me," he demanded. "I won't let you."

The elevator dinged as it halted on the lobby level.

"Good-bye, Jerry," I replied.

"I'll find you. I won't let you leave me here alone," he spat out. His words were venomous and full of menace, but they were empty. He'd never be able to leave the elevator unless he went to the next plane.

"Fuck you, Jerry," I answered levelly, marching off the elevator car as the doors slid open.

I could hear him screaming at me as I walked through the lobby and out the front doors, but I didn't look back.

Like all ghosts, he was stuck in the past and that's where I intended to leave him.

Chapter Two

As soon as I walked through the front door, Teri materialized in the living room.

"What are you doing back so early?" she asked. "You get fired or something?"

I dropped my purse on the floor and tried to hang my keys on the hook by the front door. I missed the hook and they hit the floor with a clatter. I left them there.

"Zoe?"

"Got it in one," I answered. "I was fired."

"Shit. Does this mean you're gonna move out? It's been kinda nice having someone to talk to after all these years."

Sighing, I kicked off my shoes and stripped off my jacket. "No, I have some money saved and the mortgage is low enough that it'll last me a while. Thanks to you."

Teri grinned at me. "Hey, I can't help it if everyone in town believes the rumors about this place."

She didn't know the half of it. The Kenna gossip mill insisted that six people had died in this house over the years and that it was haunted by a demon.

In reality, there had been two deaths here, but nothing like they thought. The first owner had died in her sleep at the ripe old age of ninety-five. Teri had been found hanging in the garage in an apparent suicide. She was adamant that wasn't case, that she'd been murdered. In fact, she mentioned it a lot.

Whether it was true or not, it had happened thirty years ago, so there wasn't much I could do about it.

"We should get drunk," Teri stated.

"*We* can't get drunk, Teri. You're a ghost. Ghosts don't drink."

"I know. I fucking miss it too. That and smoking." She paused. "And sex. God, do I miss sex. Do you know how difficult it is to have an orgasm when you don't have a physical form?"

I clapped my hands over my ears. "TMI! Do not tell me things like that!"

She sneered at me. "Well who am I supposed to tell? My pickings are slim for friends. You're my best friend by default."

"Oh great, so even the ghosts in this town would rather be friends with someone other than me," I quipped.

"Hey, that slutty girl likes you."

I glared at her. "Jonelle isn't slutty. She just isn't ready to settle down."

"She goes through men faster than a teenage boy goes through hand lotion."

I grimaced at her analogy. "Ick."

Teri nodded. "Yes. It's also accurate."

I shook my head and walked past her toward the kitchen. I didn't intend to get drunk but a bottle of hard cider, or two, wouldn't be unwelcome right now.

As usual, Teri was exaggerating. Jonelle did date a lot, but only because she didn't want to settle down. She wanted to enjoy her youth while she still had it...at least that's what she claimed. I had a feeling it had more to do with the fact that she didn't trust any man to stick around when the going got tough.

"Speaking of the cock hopper, you should call her."

I glared at Teri over my shoulder. "First of all, don't call her a cock hopper. Ever. Or I'll be forced to revoke your daytime TV privileges."

Teri gasped. "You wouldn't."

"I would. Secondly, why would I call Jonelle right now? It's the middle of the day, she's probably at work."

Jonelle worked at a salon in Weatherford. Fridays and Saturdays were her busiest.

My resident ghost rolled her eyes. "Because she's your best friend and she might want to know you just got canned so she can be supportive or some shit."

"I'll call her later." My phone slid across the counter toward me and I jumped, whirling to face her. "Dammit, Teri, I told you not to do stuff like that."

She smirked at me. "I'm getting better at moving things. I've been practicing."

I regretted encouraging her to interact with objects. Once Teri figured out how to move things, she liked to freak out my friends and family when they came to visit. After a couple of years, my mother refused to set foot in my house anymore.

"Call her," Teri insisted.

"Fine," I snapped, snatching up the cordless phone. I sighed, realizing I would probably have to cancel my landline soon in order to save money.

Jonelle picked up on the third ring. "Hey, girl. Are you sick?"

I hesitated. "Uh, no. Why do you ask?"

"You're calling me from your home phone at ten in the morning on a weekday," she explained.

"Oh. Um, no, I'm not sick."

"Is something else wrong?" she asked.

I sighed when I felt Teri's cold finger prod my shoulder. "Yeah. I got fired this morning."

"Damn. Did you finally lose your shit on that sneaky, thieving bitch in the cubicle next to yours?"

I huffed out a laugh. "No. They're downsizing. My office alone is cutting one hundred reps."

"And you're one of them?" Jonelle prompted.

"Yeah."

"That blows, sweetie. Are you going to be okay? Do you need some cash or anything?"

I smiled at her offer. Jonelle was such a generous friend. "I should be good. I have some money saved."

"Okay, well let me know if that changes," she stated. "I can float you a loan.

"Thanks, Jonelle."

We chatted a few more minutes, then her client arrived and Jonelle had to hang up.

I put the phone back on the charging stand and found Teri staring at me, her arms crossed over her chest.

"Feel better?"

I scowled at her. "Yes."

"Then stop frowning at me. It'll give you wrinkles."

Rolling my eyes, I grabbed my hard cider and carried it into the living room.

Teri followed me. "Well, it's ten-fifteen."

"Okaaay," I drawled in response, unsure why she was announcing the time to me.

"The firefighter next door likes to workout in his backyard this time of day."

I stared at her blankly.

"Shirtless."

I shrugged. "So?"

She shook her head in disgust. "There's no hope for you." Then she moved through the wall, her faded outline dissipating against the cool blue background.

My resident ghost was slightly obsessed with my neighbor, Preston. She'd been telling me since I'd moved in that I should ask him over for coffee or dinner. Or sex. I hadn't done either. Mostly because I thought Teri was pushing me toward my neighbor in an effort to live vicariously through me.

Also, I resisted because Preston just wasn't my type. He was a nice man in his early thirties, good-looking, and employed. All the things most women would want in a potential mate.

But he wasn't for me.

Like so many other people in the small town of Kenna, Texas, Preston Rogers thought I was...peculiar.

And for good reason.

When I was five, I died. No one could ever figure out what happened. My heart just—stopped. I was dead for nearly two minutes. The only reason I recovered was because the woman who lived across the street from us was a nurse. She saw me collapse on the front lawn and ran over to help. To this day, twenty-two years later, my mother refers to it as *the incident*.

When I regained consciousness in the hospital, I saw a man standing by the door to my room. I asked my mother who he was, but she insisted that there was no one else there.

It took me a while to realize what I was seeing. For the first few months, I told everyone I knew about the people I saw that no one else did.

As I grew older I began to understand that they were ghosts. By then it was too late, everyone in my small town thought I was more than a little off since *the incident*.

Then, in high school, I'd gone to the local cemetery with a group of kids. They dared me to go in alone. When I did, two of the fresh graves nearby opened up and out climbed a couple of corpses. Needless to say, the kids who I'd desperately wanted to befriend had left me stranded in that graveyard.

Discovering what was happening to me became vitally important. After that night, I drove to Fort Worth and spent hours poring through books about the supernatural. I assumed that the bodies I'd raised in the cemetery were zombies, but I hadn't intended for them to rise from the grave, so I doubted that I was a necromancer.

Then there were the ghouls. Once I turned eighteen, men noticed me. However, it was only certain men and their interest was borderline creepy. Okay, forget creepy, it was borderline frightening.

I didn't understand what they were until I finally confronted a young ghoul with my can of pepper spray and a whole lot of attitude. He'd stammered out an explanation of what he was, which was unsettling in itself, and then I'd asked him not to continue when he'd begun talking about how he couldn't resist me. Eating dead flesh was a massive turn off. Add in stalker tendencies, and I was ready to give him a blast of pepper spray just on principle.

Over the years, I'd stopped acknowledging my abilities. When I was a child, I constantly talked about the people only I could see and it alienated me from other kids.

I quit talking about it with my parents because my mother would freak out or loudly demand that I stop lying.

The only person who seemed to understand and accept what was happening to me was my paternal grandmother. She listened to me when I told her the stories and described what I saw.

Not long before she passed away, she said to me, "Sweetie, when you died and they revived you, I think a piece of the other side came back with your soul."

I still found those words comforting though my grandmother had been dead for seven years now.

"Oh, hell yeah! Take it off, baby!"

Teri's voice cut through my maudlin mood as she whooped and hollered. Clearly, Preston had begun his workout in his backyard.

Taking a sip of my hard cider, I picked up the TV remote and settled in to watch true crime shows.

There was a knock on my door a couple hours later. Teri had gone quiet, which was typical for her. Sometimes I wondered if she took a nap in the afternoon like a whiny toddler. Or a bitchy she-ghost.

I hauled myself off the couch, feeling more than a little tipsy. Peeking out the small windows that ran up each side of the doorjamb, I saw Jonelle standing on my front porch.

Throwing open the door, I asked, "What are you doing here?"

She grinned at me and held up a bottle of sparkling wine. "Celebrating."

Though I was half drunk, her answer still made no sense to me.

"Huh?"

She brushed by me as she entered the house. "I'm helping you celebrate moving on from that job. You've mentioned changing careers several times in the past few months. Maybe this is an opportunity."

I ignored her statement, even though it was true. "Don't you have clients?"

Jonelle shrugged, brushing her blonde hair off her shoulders. "I only had a couple. I rescheduled them for tomorrow."

"Jonelle..."

She shoved the bottle of wine at me. "Take the wine. Pour me a glass. No complaining. You've had a shitty morning and we're going to take a day to goof off."

I couldn't help but grin at her. "Yes, boss."

Nodding, she replied, "Damn skippy."

Rolling my eyes at her goofiness, I carried the wine into the kitchen. I laughed when I realized that the wine was screw top. Clearly we were going to be classy bitches and drink cheap wine.

"I see the cock hopper showed up," Teri said behind me.

I twisted around and pointed at her. "That's it. I'm leaving tomorrow for the entire day and I'm going to put Tori Amos on repeat. Do not call her that!"

"Call her what?" Jonelle asked as she walked into the room, passing right through Teri's opaque body.

Teri wailed, "Goddammit, I hate it when she does that!"

Though Jonelle swore she couldn't see Teri, I think she could at least sense her because she did that a lot.

"Teri was calling you a not-so-nice name. I was planning to punish her with *Happy Phantom* on repeat, but you just walked right through her so that may be punishment enough."

"So what did she call me?" Jonelle took the glass of wine I held out to her. When I hesitated, she sighed. "As if anything that demon poltergeist could call me would hurt my feelings."

"Cock hopper," I stated.

Jonelle choked on her wine as she guffawed. "Oh my God, that's a good one. I've got to remember that."

I turned my gaze to Teri, making sure my displeasure was clear. "Go see if Preston is still working out and we'll talk later."

Jonelle's eyebrows rose at my statement. "Preston is working out right now? Is he shirtless?"

I sighed. Though Teri seemed to despise Jonelle, they did share a common interest in my neighbor. Probably because he wouldn't have sex with either of them. He seemed skittish around Jonelle, as if she was a bomb he expected to go off at any second.

"I'll be right back," Jonelle commented, disappearing through the door. I heard her footsteps fade as she walked to the formal dining room across the hall. It had an unobstructed view into Preston's back yard.

Though their bickering required my participation and annoyed me to no end, it had accomplished the one thing I hadn't thought possible.

It took my mind off the fact that I was now unemployed.

Read it here!

About the Author

Born and raised in Texas, C.C. Wood writes saucy paranormal and contemporary romances featuring strong, sassy women and the men that love them. If you ever meet C.C. in person, keep in mind that many of her characters are inspired by people she knows, so anything you say or do is likely to end up in a book one day.

A self-professed hermit, C.C. loves to stay home, where she reads, writes, cooks, and watches TV. She can usually be found drinking coffee or a cocktail as she spends time with her hubby and daughter.

Also by C.C. Wood

Kiss Me

Westfall Brothers Series:

Texas with a Twist

Paranormal Romance:

The Witch's Gift

-

<u>**Novels:**</u>

Seasons of Sorrow

All or Nothing

Printed in Great Britain
by Amazon

30060627R00126